ABOUT THIS BOOK

Welcome to Havenwood Falls, a small town in the majestic mountains of Colorado. A town where legacies began centuries ago, bloodlines run deep, and dark secrets abound. A town where nobody is what you think, where truths pose as lies, and where myths blend with reality. A place where everyone has a story. Including the high schoolers. This is only but one . . .

Breckin Roberts has known Vivienne his entire life. Born and raised in Havenwood Falls, they attend the same school, eat at the same restaurants, and enjoy the same festivals. But they aren't friends. They're merely two classmates—her human and him not so much. Until one fateful December afternoon.

When Vivienne Freeman awakens late that night, disheveled and disoriented, the last thing she remembers is going for a run, but something feels . . . off. It's not until the gorgeous but ever elusive Breckin Roberts approaches her out of the blue that she learns she almost died. And he's the one who saved her.

Or so he thought.

Turns out, saving Vivienne has opened her to a whole new kind of danger. Breckin is an angel who interfered with Death. It's a slight easily forgiven, if not for the connection he awakens while healing her. A connection one reaper finds highly appealing. A connection that could turn Vivienne into a pawn in the battle of good versus evil—a battle about to descend on Havenwood Falls.

AWAKEN THE SOUL

A HAVENWOOD FALLS HIGH NOVELLA

MICHELE G. MILLER

HAVENWOOD FALLS HIGH BOOKS

Written in the Stars by Kallie Ross

Reawakened by Morgan Wylie

The Fall by Kristen Yard

Somewhere Within by Amy Hale

Awaken the Soul by Michele G. Miller

Bound by Shadows by Cameo Renae (Jan. 2018)

Inamorata by Randi Cooley Wilson (Feb. 2018)

More books releasing on a monthly basis

Stay up to date at www.HavenwoodFalls.com.

OTHER BOOKS BY MICHELE G MILLER

From the Wreckage Series – Coming of Age Dramas

From the Wreckage

Out of Ruins

All That Remains

West: A POV Novel

After the Fall - Austin's story (New Adult Suspense)

Into the Fire – Dani's story

The Prophecy of Tyalbrook Trilogy – YA Fantasy Romances

Never Let You Fall

Never Let You Go

Never Without You – Coming 2018

Individual titles

Last Call – New Adult Romance

CO-WRITTEN WITH MINDY HAYES

Paper Planes Standalone Series – Sweet Contemporary Romances

Paper Planes and Other Things We Lost (YA)

Subway Stops and the Places We Meet (Adult)

Chasing Cars and the Lessons We Learned (New Adult)

Nothing Compares 2 U, novella - *10 Things I Love About You Anthology*
(New Adult)

HOLD ON FOR YOUR LIFE

BRECKIN

*W*hite. Everywhere I look. Pure, undiluted, untouched. Colorado in December.

Banking left, the tip of my wing disturbs a snow-laden pine bough, scattering ice crystals. The mountain forest is peaceful this late in the afternoon, though the threat of a storm lurks in the gray sky. A gust rolls in from the north, and I snap my wings, letting the airstream guide my path toward home.

How long will this peace last? This morning's message from Elias served as an eerie reminder of my time limit. Four months. Tucking my wings, I shift, free-falling toward the ground, dodging trees as I dart in and around the woods. Freedom. I arch skyward, shooting high above Mount Alexa. The ground, the falls, the trees—they are blemishes on a snowy white canvas.

A scream penetrates the peace. I twist, levitating among the clouds, my gaze narrowing on the ground far below.

The crimson trail, smeared for yards before the dense forest covers the evidence, is hard to miss.

Blood. Thick, human blood.

This is Havenwood Falls—it's not an abnormal occurrence in the forest. But . . .

I dive, lured by a scent that burns my nostrils and confuses my senses.

I'm on the ground within moments of her scream. Her keening death cries prick at my skin, sending an unfamiliar sensation skittering up my spine and across my wings. Angry snarls join her moans. I should leave, yet I press on—following the blood trail. The creature drags her instead of making a clean kill. Most shifters kill, rather than play with, their food. I maintain distance, preferring to remain in the good graces of the other supernatural beings within Havenwood Falls. Angel or not, minding my business keeps the peace. History has proven this. The world is a better place when all creatures, good and evil, play nice together. That type of thinking will be my downfall in four months, if I'm not careful.

An unnatural calm claims the still woods, and my senses sharpen. I move forward as an ache builds up in my chest. Her cries diminish, but her scent strengthens. It's familiar. The spicy combination of ginger root and mint. I duck beneath low branches and break through thicker brush, my steps quickening as I track them. Another growl disturbs the woods, and I pause. Twenty feet ahead, a shadow of fur and menace crosses my path—retreating. The feeling in my chest intensifies like a fist crushing my heart.

Ginger, mint, and something—more. They inundate me as I maneuver around a thick tree and come to a stop.

She is bathed in blood. Her long golden hair spreads around her head, a silken halo on a snowy pillow of white. From my vantage point, I cannot see her face, but her scent—her perfume—gives her away.

Vivienne Freeman.

And above her lifeless body, he is ageless and brings with him the kiss of death. A reaper. His corporeal existence remains unseen to the human eye.

Her name begs to be spoken. A kick to the gut, it is an urge unlike any other. The image of her, two desks in front of me in chemistry for the past few months, is superimposed on the gruesome scene before me. The wisps of hair framing her face, her elegant profile, the way she hunches over her desk while she works. Movement breaks the memory. The reaper's swirling mixture of light and dark extends toward her face, and a thread of black touches her forehead reverently. The perceived intimacy compels me across snow and blood, my wings bared as a warning to this angelic host.

"Leave her be."

Reapers have no affiliation with Heaven or Hell. They're vessels of Death. Wardens sent to usher souls from this life into the next. I've had limited interaction with others of my kind, but I know about egos. I'm the son of an angel, with a human soul, thanks to the woman who gave me life. One of the Nephilim. In hierarchy alone, I win.

Dropping to my knees, I take in Vivienne's shredded jacket and blood-soaked clothing. Her face matches the snow—pale, deathly. Her lips colorless. Her heart? My hand presses against her chest. The pulse is faint, but it beats. Barely.

The reaper hisses as a ripple shocks the air, shattering the calm. His cloaked form floats back as though pushed by the disturbance. He turns, and his piercing blue eyes hold my gaze. *She is mine, son of angels.* His voice does not speak for human ears. He has no body, no face—only a mist-like outline and blue eyes.

"She isn't dead." My hands rip at her clothing, searching out her injuries.

Her heart beats. He can't kill her. Reapers don't kill. They reap souls once the earthly bodies die, nothing more. I can save her. Grabbing my sweatshirt from where I keep it tucked into my waistband when I fly, I staunch the flow of blood from her wounds. The fabric soaks through immediately. A call to medics won't help. She'll be dead in minutes.

As though he's read my mind, the reaper reaches out once again, straining for her. This is Death. I have no part in it. I barely know Vivienne. She's a classmate, not even a friend. A beautiful girl I've known my entire life, but who has never been impressed by me or my antics.

"Don't take her." The words pour from my lips as the falls pour through the rocks of Cooley Creek. "Can't you spare her? Does she have to die?"

My questions are futile. Reapers don't decide these things. There is a larger plan. We all merely follow it. My fists slam the ground. Why can't I walk away?

She is special, the reaper speaks in my mind, soft and low. *Lovely. Her soul was meant for more.*

He rambles like someone in awe. His little, obsessive words click through my head. *I want, I want, I want,* he murmurs. *So special. So different.*

Rage builds within my chest as his chattering continues. Spots flash in my vision, and my stomach hardens as bitterness coats my tongue.

"She is mine!" I shout the statement within my soul and out of my lips.

No. She is mine, son of angels.

Low, guttural anger rips from within, snapping my control. My hands burn as my muscles bunch and flex, and the world around us dims, blackness snuffing out the afternoon sun. Shadows grow long, branches creak, and the reaper drifts away once again.

I mock his pitiful presence. "Yes, I *am* the son of an angel. I do not cower before a warden of Death."

"You are a boy," the reaper says aloud, his shroud waving in the wind as the heat consuming my hands creeps up my arms.

The light of a thousand fires burns at the tips of my fingers pressed against Vivienne's wounds. *Heal her.* I call upon an ability I possess, but have never tapped into. My teeth grind in my tight jaw.

The reaper's hisses are nonstop. He is furious. I'm saving his prey, taking his prize. His electric eyes flash as he lowers to the ground and assumes an upright position, hovering above the snow. He remains nothing but spirals of mist, taking the loose shape of the classic specter of Death humans are used to visualizing.

A cold touch shocks my side, and I flinch. *Vivienne's hand.* It slides down my bare ribs, searching for purchase. Her fingers curl around a belt loop of my black jeans as her back arches off the ground. The intensity in my palms grows, and pain contorts Vivienne's features. Her brows draw above her eyes, her mouth forming a voiceless scream as a dribble of blood coats her bottom lip. Her free hand digs into the snow. Her suffering torments me, and yet I hold tight, healing her as she writhes. Her heels scrape against the wet ground as her legs bend and stretch. She's missing one running shoe.

Then it's done.

The light dies. The weak, gray sun reappears.

Vivienne's eyes flutter, offering little glimpses of watery blue nirvana before they close, and her head falls to the side.

With a smug grin, I lift my gaze to the reaper.

I want her, he says with his mind, his eyes.

My lip curls. "You can't have her."

I will. His black head tilts, a subtle nod, then he's gone.

The forest awakens, the calm of death no longer holding life at a standstill.

My coarse breaths come quickly, my pulse racing as I gather Vivienne close. Leaning over her, I press my lips to the frozen edge of her ear. "It's okay. I've got you. You're safe."

Her heart beats, strong and steady.

My muscles relax as I survey the forest. It's nearly nightfall. The temperature dropped rapidly in the last several minutes. The air is ripe with the scent of the gathering storm. It's a mile, possibly two, north. Tucking my ruined sweatshirt between our bodies, I search the ground for evidence of what transpired here. Her blood is everywhere, but nothing else. The storm will cover the blood from human eyes, although the scent will drive the supernaturals in town crazy. Nothing to be done right now. I need to move Vivienne someplace warm.

Cradling her close, I leap into the air and snap my wings wide. I'll take her to my house, clean her up, and make sure she's okay. I'll figure out my next move after that.

Unanswered questions bombard me. *What happened in the forest? Why did I react with such savagery? Will the reaper be back? Should I worry? Tell Elias? Speak to Father?* No. I won't call upon him. I have four months, six if I can convince him to let me finish out school, before I take my place at his side. His or another's—the decision has yet to be made, and I need all the time away from him I can get.

My forehead lowers, pressing to Vivienne's temple as my hands tighten their grip. Her lips have regained a pink, human tone. I inhale a shaky breath as the emptiness, the nothingness, I've lived with disappears. She replaced it in an instant. Her scent fills me. Her warmth, her life, digs into my soul with gripping talons, anchoring in and refusing to let go. These emotions are unexpected and unwanted. I've never felt much of anything for anyone.

Is this feeling human or angelic?

THE FIRST SNOWFLAKES appear before I reach home. Staying low, I fly above the tree line and cloak us from sight as we soar over Havenwood Heights. If I were alone, I'd be home already, a perk of angelic birth, but Vivienne is vulnerable. Especially in her current state. Her pulse remains strong, her heartbeat steady, but her color is pallid. She lost too much blood, and I don't know how my healing abilities work. *Should I take her to the medical center? Her mom works there, but what would I say? Maybe I should bring her home?* The feathers between my shoulder blades twitch. *Yeah, I'm not a fan of that idea either.*

We land on my back deck, and I head straight for the nearest guest room. Forcing my arms to cooperate, I release Vivienne onto the bed as I shift pillows beneath her damp head. I carefully work off her bloody jacket, ruined shoe, and wet socks. She's dressed in athletic gear —thick, waterproof running pants, a sweatshirt, a thermal—and it's all ruined by blood. She'll have to forgive me for the skin I see as I rip at her shirts. Her side is injury free. Smeared blood and mottled bruising the only proof anything happened.

Clenching my jaw, my fingers slip into the waistband of her pants and work them down her hips. At the sight of her running tights, I release a relieved breath. I leave them on—they're clean, dry, and modest. When I finish, I sweep the dirty comforter away and cover her with a thick blanket. My fingers linger at her temple as I brush her hair from her face. Her skin is warmer. And soft. So damn soft. It's an effort to remove my hand and leave the room.

Once in my room, I swipe my hands through my hair and curse. Even from across the house, she tugs at me, wanting me to return. I press my palm to my chest as though I can press her out. *What is going on?* I change into clean sweats and a T-shirt, splash my face with cold water, and head for the kitchen, my thoughts on making Vivienne something warm, when my cell goes off.

The screen flashes: Elias.

"Hey man," I answer nonchalantly.

"Hey man?" Accusation laces his words.

Crap.

"Your silence is telling. What happened?"

Did he notice it, too? The bizarre shift in the air, the release of my abilities, the reaper's presence? "To what are you referring?"

I stick a milk-filled mug in the microwave.

"I've suspended service for the night. Should I come over? Or call your father?" he asks meaningfully.

"I used my abilities." I slam a cabinet shut. "It was unintentional."

A tirade of colorful curses serenades me. "Tell me what happened."

"I don't know." I chew on my lip and contemplate my words. "There was a reaper."

Okay then, forget a well-thought-out explanation. Let's lead with the biggie.

"A reaper?" Elias repeats. "Who died?"

"No one."

"No one?" His breath hitches. "You healed? Why in the hell would you do that?"

His anger raises my hackles. "Because I can."

"Breckin."

"Don't lecture me, Elias. I need to go. I'll explain everything later." I end the call and toss my phone on the counter.

When I return to Vivienne, she's on her side with one hand resting beneath her cheek and the other clutching a down blanket to her chest. The thick bedding swallows her. She's tiny, a foot shorter and seventy-five pounds lighter than me. The weight of her in my arms lingers.

Splotches of red mar her fingers and smear her chin. Leaving her drink on the bedside table, I head toward the bathroom and return with a warm washcloth. I'm aware of each swipe of the cloth, like I'm washing my own hands. Vivienne sighs and flinches when I set her hand down and rub her jaw. A whimper releases from her throat, making me pause.

She brushes her chin against her shoulder as she shifts restlessly. Her forehead creases as she fists the blankets and draws the edge to her mouth, tucking her face in before settling down.

The wind howls as a thick veil of white comes down fast outside my windows. I move from the edge of the bed to a chair across the room, my heart slowing as hers does, and I wait. There's nothing more I can do.

BAD DREAM

VIVIENNE

*S*lapping at my bedside table, my hand searches for the incessant vibration dragging me unwillingly from sleep. Finding my cell phone, I fumble with the screen, bringing the device to my ear. "Hello?" I clear my throat and repeat myself when the word barely passes my lips.

"Viv? Where have you been?" Mom's voice sounds far, far away. I blink rapidly, clearing the sleep from my brain. "Were you asleep, honey? I've been calling all evening. Are you sick?"

Her questions come in quick-fire succession, and I struggle to keep up while sitting. Rubbing my aching temple, I peek at my cell for the time. Midnight. What the heck?

"Uh . . . no. Or, yeah. Yeah, I was sleeping. I'm not sick. Just tired."

There's a pause. A shift on the other end. "You didn't call after your run. You know you're supposed to let me know when you get home if I'm not there. I was worried. Especially with this storm raging and the disappearance of the Bennett girl."

Heidi Bennett. She went missing last weekend, during the Cold Moon Ball. The adults around town are freaking out, but consensus at school is she probably had a fight with her boyfriend, or parents, and

9

will show up in a few days. I work my head side to side, stretching out the kinks as I wait for her to say more.

"Viv? Are you sure everything is okay?"

"Mmmhmmm," I hum, focusing on a shadow lurking beyond my window. The hair on the back of my neck stands. I never leave my blinds and curtains open, especially at night. Living on the first floor of an apartment complex doesn't offer a whole lot of privacy. Plus, the guys across the way are pervs. "Yeah. I'm fine. Sorry I didn't call. I laid down. I guess I fell asleep."

After your run. Her words register belatedly, and my pulse picks up.

"Okay, sweetie. Go back to sleep, and I'll see you when I get home in the morning."

I nod, then remember I'm on the phone. "Yeah, okay, have a good shift. Love you."

"I went for a run," I say to the empty room after the call ends.

The snow outside reflects the bright winter moon and casts long shadows across my small bedroom. Sinking into my blankets, I pull my comforter over my bare shoulders. *Wait. Bare shoulders?* My hands run over my body. *What am I wearing? Running tights and a sports bra?* Kicking into a sitting position, I draw my knees to my chest.

I went for a run. I . . . Tears prick my eyes.

A dark flash hurtles at me. Pain. Blood. My throat closes. *No. It was a dream. A nightmare.*

Hurrying from my room, I search for my clothing. My jacket, pants, shoes, any of the gear I normally wear running. I flip on lights, search closets, the hampers, the washing machine. My heart plays the beat of a thousand drums.

A low, animalistic snarl fills my ears. A cool touch. An urgent voice. My knees give way, and I crumble to the floor, dizzy and spent. *Why can't I remember anything? What am I missing? Nothing is right.* I crawl to the couch and pull myself up, drawing a throw over my body. I need sleep. Maybe I am getting sick.

The view from the couch to my bedroom window is unhindered, and there—beside the pine outside my building—is a shadow.

My eyelids grow heavy as I peer across the apartment. A shadow in the form of a human.

I pry my eyes wider, my temples pounding. A shadow with amber eyes.

I should be scared by a shadow outside my window in the middle of the night. I should call 911, I should scream, but I don't. I'm not afraid. My mind calms as my frantic heart settles. With one last sleepy effort, I search out the shadow, catching a wavering glimpse before everything falls dark.

"You're bloody crazy, Viv." Zara blows into her cupped hands as she shifts from foot to foot.

"Are you being British again?" I laugh as I walk the steps from my window to the pine for the third time. My gaze searches the ground for something—anything—that proves someone stood out here last night. "Which Austen movie did you watch yesterday?"

"It wasn't Austen. It was a documentary on the royal family. It was brilliant."

"You're mad." Though I'm teasing, I can't help but go into character and pull out my British slang.

"Well done." Zara's tone and accent come out a bit Mary Poppins. Her fascination with British culture knows no end. We've spent thousands of hours watching, listening to, and studying British entertainment. "But, I would argue I am not the one here who is insane, my dear Viv."

"I know what I saw. Someone was out here last night."

"And in your apartment, stealing your clothes?" She steps into the snow and works her way to my side. "There is nothing here. Even if you did have a Peeping Tom, there would be no evidence. It snowed all night. You're not going to find a fresh set of footprints. You've watched too many crime shows."

Why did I bother telling her?

Zara tugs her knit hat over her ears, smooshing down her thick, dark hair. "Can we go inside? I'm freezing and you don't have a jacket on."

"That's because I can't find my jacket," I remind her.

"Did you tell your mum?"

Grabbing her arm, I lead her toward the apartment. "Tell her what? That someone robbed me of my running gear? That I'm seeing things?"

I'm positive something happened yesterday. Something bad. Something dangerous. I rack my brain for any semblance of what it could have been.

A smattering of needles prick across my shoulders, and I pause, my gaze scanning the parking lot, looking for something, sensing it. Other than the kids building a snowman by the building across from mine, the complex is quiet.

"Mom's already giving me a hard time about running alone since Heidi went missing. If I alert her to anything out of the ordinary, she'll start making me spend all my free time at the medical center with her."

"Good point." Zara weaves her arm beneath mine. "Let's go. We can drive over to Backwoods and buy you a new coat before the movie."

"THIS IS NOT how I intended spending the last of my birthday money," I complain as I dig for my wallet and hand most of my cash to Willa Kasun, who smiles sympathetically from behind the register.

"The fact that you still have birthday money from last April is telling, my friend," Zara, the spendthrift, says with a shake of her head.

The snap of a shopping bag opening draws me from my pouting. "Oh, actually, can you remove the tags so I can wear it?" Willa's dark brow arches. "I lost mine, and it's a bit chilly out there without one."

Zara nudges my shoulder, an inelegant snort jerking her shoulders. "She's so daft. She'd misplace her arse if it weren't attached."

Daft? I mouth, giving my so-called best friend a fixed look.

Willa's lips twitch as she pulls out a pair of scissors, cuts the tags, and slides my new jacket across the counter with the receipt on top.

"Thanks. See ya." I toss a wave as she gives me her canned "Thanks for shopping at Backwoods Sport & Ski."

Shoving Zara toward the exit, I hiss, "Way to go, Z. She probably thinks I'm a complete idiot."

Zara giggles and stops at a sunglass display. She slides a gaudy red and gold pair on and poses. "Whatever. No one thinks you're an idiot. We go to the same school; she knows you're Ms. Academia. Plus, she shared a womb with Kase. She most certainly knows an idiot when she sees one."

"Oh my gosh, shut up." I swallow back a giggle and search the immediate area, clamping down on her arm. The Kasuns own this store. Their dad is sheriff, their older brothers are deputies, and Kase—while not the sharpest pencil in the box—is well-known and well-liked. "Besides, I know for a fact you're smitten with him."

"Smitten?" Zara's light caramel skin flushes as she smirks. "I am not smitten. He's hot, I'll give him that, but after that mess with Ana? No, thank you. I'm staying far, far away from him."

"You have excellent self-preservation skills. They may be over, but Ana would rip your head off if she thought you were after him."

A deep chuckle nearby stops me. I turn, blood creeping up my neck at being overheard, but there's no one there. The store's busy enough, locals and tourists alike flipping through the racks of ski gear and sporting goods, but not one of them pays us a bit of attention. No smiles, no curious eyes. I adjust my scarf, pulling it around my neck as goosebumps appear across my skin.

"Pizza or burgers?" Zara asks as we step outside and I shrug into my jacket. I lift a shoulder, my mind occupied with the eerie sensations crawling over my skin. Everything within me screams in warning, and like last night, nothing is right.

"You said burgers, right?" she prods and bats her large Bambi eyes.

It's a standing joke—what's for dinner? Zara works at Napoli's. She always wants Burger Bar when we go out. I prefer Napoli's, probably because they prepare me special orders since they're used to me hanging around. Shaking away the pall hanging over me, I agree to burgers. I'm in no mood to argue.

"Burgers it is." She swings her keyring around her index finger and heads for the parking lot. I glance back at the store one last time before following.

There are a few cars parked at the drive-in bays outside the Burger Bar, but the inside is packed. The crowded booths and occupied tables aren't a surprise. Some of the girls from school wave us over and share their booth.

Living in Havenwood Falls is like living in a fishbowl. We breathe the same air and walk the same paths daily. We see the same people at every restaurant, movie showing, and festival. It's the second Saturday of the month—movie night. It's been a Havenwood Falls tradition since long before my birth. It began as a summer ritual, a family-friendly movie in Danzan Park, but once the Arts Council renovated the old mining warehouse—adding a stage and theater—the city extended the showings to year-round. Havenwood Falls, known for strange occurrences and more festivals than days of the week, is heaven for a people watcher like me.

Dipping my fries in a pile of peppered mayo, I half listen to the girls chat about their day on the slopes while my gaze flits over the crowded restaurant. I'm entertained by the guys at the next table as they jostle one another over a ketchup bottle. No need to question why I've never seen them with dates. Poor immature fools.

Across the restaurant, Nikki Morris fusses with her perfect hair and makes faces at her phone. I can't tell whether she is taking a selfie or using the camera as a mirror. The new kid, Max Cooper, arrives, and she straightens, plastering on a glowing smile and lowering her cell. I'm happy they're still dating after all the mess she's been in lately. They're both insanely good-looking, like many of the people in Havenwood Falls, and popular. I turn my head, my gaze sliding past holiday decorations covering every vacant spot in the restaurant, before they stop on a vaguely familiar face. He's propped against the wall next to the entrance with a menu in his hands, but his eyes aren't reading the daily specials. They're firmly set on me.

Intensely charged blue orbs framed by dark lashes and a pale face — *Wait.* I blink nervously. My eyes and mind play tricks on me. I don't know him at all, yet my pulse ratcheted up the moment I spotted him. Flickers of memories tickle the back of my mind, knocking and asking to be let in.

My lungs deflate, each breath more difficult than the last, the longer he stares. I grip the table, my fingers curling around the metal edge, as a chill creeps up my spine. He pushes from the wall, and I lurch forward.

Zara jumps, her hands grabbing the cup of water I knocked over. "What the hell, Viv?"

She pushes my shoulder while across the table, the others shift baskets and throw napkins on the mess I've made.

"Sorry. I don't know what happened. I—"

"You were totally eye screwing that guy, that's what happened. Who is he?" Zara nudges my side again. "You're soaked. Get up, you loon."

"I'm—" *Soaked?* Cold moisture seeps through my jeans, and I look down as water dribbles off the table into my lap.

"Yep, I'm wet," I say lamely, sliding from the booth.

"What guy?" the girls ask in tandem as their heads swivel in the direction of the door.

He's gone.

"Viv?" Zara touches my hand at my side. "Are you okay? You're shaking."

My head nods of its own accord as I will my trembling to cease and look over the restaurant. People laugh, people eat, everything's the same. Except for the guy, who is no longer by the door. I tug at the sleeves of my sweater.

"I'm fine. Um, I'm gonna go to the bathroom. I'll be back."

Faint voices tap at the back of my head, like gnats flying around on a summer day. They buzz and swoop close, only to retreat—taking whatever secrets they hold with them. The sensation makes me dizzy as

I round the corner to the bathroom and pull up in time to miss bumping into Scarlet Howe. Scarlet smiles and holds her hands up like I'm a robber as I apologize and press against the wall so she can pass. I take three steps backward and turn for the door handle when someone grabs my wrist and yanks me into the bathroom.

"Don't scream," a voice says as the light flicks on in the single-person restroom, and he spins my back to the wall.

My scream dies when I see Breckin Roberts standing over me, his face so close his breath caresses my cheek. My entire body lights up like a Christmas tree. A spark of something—awareness?—slips across his face, and his head cocks to the side. Gosh, I could stare at him all night. I want to. Just stand right here and look at him.

"You need to come with me." His tone leaves no room for questions, so of course, I scoff.

"Are you high? This is the girls' restroom, Breckin."

"I need you to come with me," he says again, as if I didn't hear him the first time.

"You want me to come with you? Is this your way of asking me out?"

What a ridiculous question. Breckin Roberts would never ask me out. Breckin doesn't ask anyone out. He skulks in corners as girls flock to him. Not that I've been watching him or anything. I attempt stepping sideways, but his palms slap on either side of my body, caging me. Something within me springs forward, reaching for him.

"Did you see him?" Breckin dips his head until our eyes are level, which is a feat, considering our one-foot height difference. Any attempt at words dies on my lips. "Did you?"

The urgency in his voice stirs the gnats to circling again. My eyes burn. *The blue eyes, the dark presence.* My jaw trembles. Where is this fear coming from?

"Hey." Breckin scans my face. "I've got you." He rubs the length of my upper arms, his touch light.

Time stops.

It's okay. I've got you. You're safe.

"What? What did you say?" The echo of a growl haunts me.

Breckin tilts his head, his teeth tugging at his bottom lip. A phantom pain slashes across my side as the image of a hand clawing at snow breaks through my mind. Gasping, I clutch my stomach. "I need to go."

I push at his chest, my words a mere whisper as blood pounds in my ears, but he stands his ground.

Breckin shakes his head, his golden-brown hair falling over his flawless face. "I can't let you go, Vivienne."

His tone is one I've never heard from him. This is Breckin. He usually drawls every syllable he says as though he couldn't care less about what he's saying or to whom he's speaking. I've always had the impression that he's honoring us with his words when he speaks. This is different. This is authority.

DON'T CLOSE YOUR EYES

BRECKIN

The color leaches from Vivienne's delicate face as her shoulders roll forward, making her appear tinier than she is. She drops her head, her long hair forming a curtain and closing her face off from my gaze.

"What happened yesterday afternoon?" Her voice cracks as she wraps her arms across her stomach. "What did you do to me?"

The moment I touched her and pulled her into the bathroom, I longed for more. More of her skin beneath mine, more of her scent, more of her presence. A spark ignited. Desperate, my fingers tangle in her blond strands, pushing them back. "I don't know what you're talking about."

Vivienne grabs my wrist, holding my hand to the side of her head.

"You're lying." Her head remains bowed as her gaze lifts until she stares at me through thick, dark lashes. My thumb brushes her temple as she speaks. "Something happened to me. You were there. That guy —" She cocks her head toward the restaurant. "He was there. I feel it. I know it."

"Viv—"

"Tell me the truth, or let me go." Fear clings to her words the way perfume clings to her body. Her fear takes root deep within me, urging my angelic side to protect her. Her scent, though . . . that damn minty ginger scent. It digs into my soul and makes me oh so human.

There are rules in Havenwood Falls. Rules governing the supernatural. There are rules with Father. I fear his rules more than the Court's.

I speak the truth regardless.

"You were attacked." My arms drop as I move back a half step.

"Attacked?" Uncertainty clouds her face. She wets her lips and swallows. "By what?"

Bear, dragon, mountain lion, wolf—you name it, it could have attacked her. A shifter or an animal with no supernatural tendencies. *Sure, Breck, while you're at it, why don't you scare the hell out of her and mention vampires, demons, and witchcraft, too?*

"If I had to guess, I'd say a small bear." Cubs aren't too scary. It's reasonable.

"A bear? In December?" She scowls.

"Right. Maybe a wolf or fox? I didn't see it. I heard you scream, and by the time I found you, it was gone and—" My explanation ends there.

"I was out for a run. I didn't see it." She tugs at her sweater sleeves, pulling them over her fists. "I don't remember anything. I just, I woke up and—" She clears her throat, changing her tone and line of questioning. "I screamed, and you just happened to be nearby?"

"I was." Her nose scrunches as a dubious little twist of her mouth appears. I raise a brow. "You're not the only person who enjoys exercising in the woods, you know."

"So, what did you do?"

There's no escaping the ego that tugs a smile across my lips. "I saved you."

She inhales through her nose, her shoulders lifting as a hand moves to her side. Her fingers brush her ribs where she was injured. "My clothes?"

"Ruined."

The door knob jiggles behind Vivienne's back, followed by two knocks. She steps away, glancing at me before looking to the door. I still—waiting for her next move.

"Someone's in here," she says after a moment, and I release a relieved breath.

She's not running. It's a start. The reaper is nearby. His imprint, much like Vivienne's fear, is detectable in the air—a unique marker with the sole purpose of notifying other angels of Death's presence. He is nearby, and he shouldn't be. He should have left Havenwood Falls, or moved on to the next soul in need of reaping. He shouldn't be lingering around Vivienne. The way he looked at Vivienne, the possessive hunger in his gaze . . . Anger spreads across my shoulders, and I roll them, forcing my wings to remain concealed.

Vivienne closes the gap between us, her head tilting back. "Why did you save me?"

If only I knew. "Why wouldn't I?"

"We're not friends, Breckin. Granted, we're not enemies, but you've never given me a reason to believe you're the knight-in-shining-armor type."

"But I've given you a reason to think I'm not?" Her comment affects me. I'm not one who is affected by humans. It matters none to me, yet I ask for clarification anyway. "That's what you think of me?" She moves back, her head high, her eyes searching for answers she will not find, and I move forward. "You know so little of me, but you think I'd leave someone for dead in the woods?"

Her feet still. She sways, her jaw dropping. "I was dying?"

The answer is in her head. It's all there. Hints of the afternoon, still frames of the horror. They wait for her to recall them fully, because swiping her memory didn't work as it should have. The moment she looked through her window last night and her eyes connected with mine, I knew it hadn't worked. I was cloaked. She shouldn't have seen or sensed my presence. She heard me laugh at her joke at the store. She felt my presence when I should have been invisible.

She awakens emotions and instincts I've never known. Something happened between us yesterday. I need answers, which means speaking to Father or Elias. And that means having her come with me, because I'll be damned if I'm leaving her out in the open for a reaper to stalk.

"Was I dying?" she asks for a second time, her hand grabbing a fistful of my shirt.

My gut twists. "You were basically dead, Viv."

Her head shakes, refusing my words, as her lips tremble and tears form on her dark lashes. "I don't understand. I don't—"

My wings tear at my back, itching for release, and I grit my teeth, holding myself together. "Come with me, and I'll explain."

"I can't walk out of here with you. I have friends out there, waiting. I'm supposed to go to the movie festival tonight."

She's right. It's not as though most of the people out there don't know me. The place is filled with kids from school and other locals. There's no reason Vivienne and I couldn't be friendly, but I'm not friendly. It's not my MO, and her friends would question her endlessly. The fewer questions, the better. I could cloak us, and we could walk out of here together, but that would still leave her friends guessing.

My mind grapples for a solution. "Doesn't your mom work night shift at the clinic? Is she working tonight?"

"Yeah. She's always on shift, since Dr. Nance died."

"Good. I want you to go out there and tell them you don't feel well, and you're going to see your mom. Tell them to go to the movies without you. I'll wait here for a minute, then sneak out and meet you by the front door."

Vivienne twists her hair over her shoulder and backs into the door. "This is crazy. You're crazy."

"Trust me."

Forcing my hands not to reach for her, I wait as she considers my request. I sense her fear and hear the anxious beating of her heart, but beneath that is more. There's an acceptance, a light, hiding behind the darkness.

She cocks her head and grabs a strand of hair, twisting it. "You'll explain everything?"

"Everything I can." Not a total lie.

Agreeing, Vivienne peeks into the hallway before giving me a look over her shoulder and slipping out the door. I immediately make myself invisible and follow. Skirting around tables and patrons, I head for the exit, all while keeping an eye on Vivienne and her friends. My sensitive hearing picks up their conversation.

"I got sick in the bathroom," she says weakly as she stands at the end of the table. "You guys should go to the movies without me. I'm gonna go see my mom."

"I'll drive you over." The offer comes from Zara, who's already sliding out of the booth. She holds Vivienne's jacket out to her.

"No," Vivienne says with too much force. "I mean, it's practically next door. I'll walk. It's fine. Plus, if I have the flu, I don't want you to get sick."

"Viv?"

"I need to go," Vivienne interrupts, grabbing her bag and cell phone. "I'll text you."

A chorus of goodbyes follow as she heads my way, and I slip out the door before she reaches me, shifting back to visible and smacking into two guys from school.

"What the hell, Breckin? Where did you. . ." Their words fade as I grab their arms, implanting an alternate memory and sending them on their way as Vivienne appears.

A rush of energy washes over me at the sight of her. It's exhilarating and confusing as hell. Most days, the two entities that make up who I am are separate, but more and more, my angelic side takes over. As my divine abilities strengthen, my humanity fades.

Vivienne makes me human.

She bites her lip when she spots me, then glances back over her shoulder, and my chest expands. I've all but lost the ability to feel over the past few years. Father hates humans—except when he wants them for satisfying his basic desires. He's deemed them useless. It's an attitude I picked up. I assumed my angel side felt indifference. It doesn't. Not with her.

"You okay?" I ask, holding out my hand.

She lifts the strap of her bag over her head, bringing it across her chest, and shoves her hands in her jacket pockets as she looks about.

It's Saturday night, and the drive-in and parking lot are full of people coming and going. The reaper's presence remains strong out here.

"Where's your truck?"

Dropping the hand I'm still holding out to her like a fool, I turn and head around the back of the building. "We don't need it."

"We don't need—" Vivienne's boots crunch the gravel and snow as she follows. "Where are you going? Breckin?"

I duck behind the fence hiding the restaurant's dumpsters.

She grumbles low, too low for human cars, but I hear every word. "What am I doing? Breckin Roberts graces me with his attention, and suddenly I'm swooning and following him into dark alleys, taking his word as gospel. I'm mental, truly mental."

"Breckin?" she hisses, coming around the fence.

"Hold on tight," I warn, and Vivienne screams as my arms go around her waist and we jump into the air. Her face tucks into my neck, a second scream vibrating against my skin as her feet kick at the air.

"Viv, it's okay. I won't let anything happen to you." My hand shifts up her back, pressing her closer to my chest. "By the way, I don't believe that qualified as an alley, and you're not mental."

Vivienne moans. "We're . . . we're . . ." She whimpers again, her anxiety skyrocketing.

"Flying?" I provide helpfully.

She whines.

"Open your eyes, Vivie," I tease, slowing our ascent. Her head shakes beneath my chin, and I chuckle at her mumbled plea. "I already said you're not crazy, and no, you're not dreaming. You're safe, I promise." Lowering my lips to her ear, I whisper, "Open your eyes."

Her arms tense—one around my neck, the other around my back. Her hand moves dangerously close to the joint of my wings and spine as she adjusts her body and lifts her head. Her face is a hair's breadth from my lips as her chin tips up and her eyes open. Fear reflects at me.

"You're wearing some sort of jet pack, right? I've seen those invention shows. The military make them, and rich people buy them as toys. You're rich, your dad travels the world . . . he brings you expensive toys—" Her high-pitched rambling draws another smile to my lips. If she'd stop talking, she'd hear the beat of my wings against the air. She continues.

"Don't drop me, Breckin. I'm not sure I'm a fan of this. I prefer driving. You have a cool vehicle, a classic even. Couldn't we have driven? Can you put me down? I mean, can we go back down?" I shift, turning my body under hers as we head east, toward my house. Vivienne squeals, squeezing her eyes closed. "No, no, no. What are you doing? How high are we? Please tell me this is a nightmare. This isn't real. You're not here, I'm in bed—"

I kiss her.

It's a simple brush of my lips against hers—one I must rip myself away from, because *holy hell*, I want more—but she shuts up.

"Was that not real?" I ask, winding my leg around her calf and locking her closer.

Her jaw works back and forth. "It couldn't have been."

We glide on the wind, my wings beating once every twenty feet. "Why not?"

She draws a shaky breath, her hand shifting at my spine, her nails digging into my skin as she clutches tighter. Her lips form a silent O.

"You're shirtless," Vivienne accuses.

It took her this long to notice? Removing my shirts when I fly is a must, unless I want to shop for new clothes every time my wings make an appearance and rip them in two.

"I am." She tilts her head, though she still doesn't look down. "I'm not wearing a jetpack, either. All you have to do is look beyond my face, and all your questions will be answered."

"Oh, I highly doubt that." Wry humor clings to her words. Catching her bottom lip with her front teeth, her eyes slide left and go wide. I still, allowing her a good look at my wings. Her chest expands with her deep inhale.

"They're real," I say preemptively. "Not some expensive toy my father bought me."

"You have wings." The rhythm of her racing heart tugs at my

angelic senses. My palm aches to press against her chest, to memorize the song each beat creates. Blood rushes to her face, and I grin.

"You like them."

Her head whips around, her blush deepening. "They're beautiful," she admits. "But I don't—"

"Crap." A dark shadow circles a hundred yards behind us. I should have caught his presence sooner. Vivienne has me off my game. "Close your eyes and hold on tight."

I push her head to my chest and bank left, flying toward Mount Alexa and over the falls. We pick up speed as I lead the reaper away from my house and the town. The Court of the Sun and the Moon would not look favorably on a Saturday night fight between angels in the square. Searching out a spot, I locate a small clearing in the trees deep in the forest, near the northernmost ridge, and land.

Vivienne's legs give out as her feet hit the snow. I loosen my hold, giving her room to stand on her own.

"What's wrong? What is it?"

I push her toward a wide tree. *How do I explain what she needs to know?*

"He's here," Vivienne says as her cold fingers clutch my bicep. Her sharp intake of breath tells me she's putting pieces together. "He has wings, too," she says, looking over my shoulder.

Deep rolling laughter sounds behind me. I turn and face the reaper, who's taken the shape of an unfamiliar teenage boy.

My hand tightens around Vivienne's. "You can't take her."

"Can't I?" His eyes flick over our heads. A snap reverberates through the forest as branches twist and break above us. We dodge to the right as a pile of snow and bark land in our footprints.

"You would kill her?" That's not allowed. Reapers do not determine death. He risks the wrath of a guardian angel; he risks the wrath of *me*. Fury builds. "You do not want to play with me, reaper."

He slinks forward. "You stole her from me."

I push Vivienne behind me. "And I would do it again."

FALLEN ANGEL

VIVIENNE

*A*ngels growl.

This little tidbit pops into my mind as the man with glowing blue eyes snarls.

Angels.

At least, I suppose that's what Breckin is—an angel.

The ground spins, and I focus on the dark wing sheltering me. My wide eyes follow the copper-tipped feathers to where they connect with Breckin's spine. They were iridescent in the moonlight, but in the shadows of the woods, they're inky black perfection against glowing skin. The impulse to stroke them is maddening.

"You cannot protect her forever, son of angels."

Breckin's wings twitch.

I slide closer, touching his lower back as he laughs. "Now, I'm sure you're familiar enough with our kind to know your challenge will not be taken lightly."

Cringing at Breckin's snide tone, I step sideways for a better look at the angel threatening us. Breckin's wing blocks me, extending like a wall. My stomach flutters at his protectiveness. *This is not the Breckin Roberts I know.*

"She is such a pretty thing. Do you plan on making her your toy?"

Breckin's muscles flex beneath my fingertips, as a hair-raising snarl vibrates in his chest. "Do you plan on dying today, reaper?"

There's the Breckin I know. Why am I suddenly finding him hot? Well, he's always been hot, but now he's Channing Tatum wearing a welding mask hot.

The other angel grunts. I lift on my toes, but Breckin is too tall, and his wings are too effective at blocking my view.

"What is your allegiance, boy? A son of angels in love with a human? They will kill you once they find out. I will take her soul from you soon enough."

A gust sprays fine snow as my breath catches. *In love with a human? My soul?* Breckin steps forward, allowing me a glimpse of this other angel. His wings, smaller and lighter in color compared to Breckin's black ones, stir the air. He levitates before us, and his wings still, as though he was merely waiting to catch my gaze. When he does, it's as though he sees through me. His eyes hold me captive.

"Do not let the half-breed taint that soul of yours, my sweet."

"Who are you? What do you want?"

Breckin grabs my wrist. "Vivienne."

I stop. I've stepped in front of Breckin—and don't recall moving.

"Soon enough." The dark angel smiles. Cool, finger-like strokes cross my mind—caressing, invading—and I stagger back, my hand against my forehead, as he shoots into the sky.

Transfixed, I stare after him, anticipating his return. Moonlight, stars, and wisps of clouds hover above the trees. No shadow angel. No blue eyes.

"Viv?" Breckin cuts through my haze. He cups my shoulder, and tingles race along my arm.

"What is this, Breckin?" My sanity hangs by a thread as questions tumble forth. "You're an angel? He's an angel? He wants to kill me? Tried to? How did you steal me from him? What's going on?"

"You're shivering." Breckin steps forward—his wings lowering and folding closer to his body—as I move back.

"I'm fine. Answer my questions."

"I will, once you're warm."

I can't see his face in the shadows of the trees, but I can read his voice. He's concerned, which is funny, considering his lack of clothing. "You're shirtless."

He releases a strangled laugh, shaking his head. "Yes, I am. I'm also not prone to hypothermia."

"Because you're an angel?" I prod.

Breckin sighs, his warm breath sending a puff of smoky air between us. "Part angel, yes."

Part angel. *Half-breed.*

I sniff, my nose running, thanks to the cold. Flexing my stiff fingers, I look about. We're high on the mountain. The air is thin, the trees scarce, the wind gusts consistent— how did I not notice this before?

Taking advantage of my preoccupation, Breckin's wings surround me, drawing me near as he bridges the gap between us. He's taller than me. Tall enough for me to fit under his chin as I walk into his arms and press my cheek against his unnaturally warm skin. My fingers lock behind his back, and he leaps at my icy touch. His dark wings envelop me—a Breckin cocoon, of sorts—and an overwhelming mix of tranquility and trepidation washes over me. Being in his arms is so right, yet I'm terrified. Not of him, or what he is—but of what's happening. I fight the pull coaxing me to stroke his wings as his feathers ruffle. His hands shift on my back, one low and one high, his fingers slipping under the hair at my nape and holding my head against his chest.

"Please don't drop me."

"I've got you."

A rush of cold air hits me, stealing my ability to reply, as we shoot into the sky.

This time I'm brave enough to turn my head and open my eyes to the world below. The lights of Havenwood Falls glow. It's a cheery, lit-up town in an otherwise dark canyon of mountains and trees. Mathews River shimmers from one end of town to the other, and beyond. Cars dot the streets, moving slowly from work to home, from homes to stores. From here, the moonlight turns the flecks of gold in

Stuart Fountain into glowing dancing fairies. The gazebo in town square is a beacon thanks to all the Christmas lights wrapped around it. My world is so small, so peaceful from this vantage point. Breckin's wing shifts into my sightline, and with a deep breath, I understand: my world is nothing like I thought.

WE CIRCLE THE TOWN TWICE—"TO assure we're not being followed," Breckin says tightly—before descending to a snow-covered deck. Breckin's house is a completely updated and remodeled historic Victorian located on the corner of Fairchild and Eleventh. Not exactly the most private spot for a family of angels. The fence around the yard is a stone wall and iron bars. Anyone who passes by can see us standing here. I would have expected them to live up in the woods on a private lot, or in Havenwood Heights. I've passed this street hundreds of times. How did I not know he lived here?

"You're not worried about people seeing you?"

Breckin shrugs as his wings disappear before my eyes, and he pulls his shirt from where it's tucked into the back of his pants and draws it over his head. "Humans don't see us like this."

"I see you," I counter, leaning this way and that for a glimpse of his back as his shirt covers his skin.

Amber eyes lock on mine. "I let you."

My argument dies, my breath catching at the cocky arch of his brow. I allow Breckin to lead me inside, his fingers warming mine. He pushes a hand through his hair, releasing deep sighs as we walk through the richly decorated—and unusually dark—house and down a set of stairs. He flips a switch, and we end up in what might as well be called an apartment in his basement. A living room, complete with a stone fireplace, a huge projection screen, and dark leather couches and chairs, fills the right side. An eat-in kitchen and bar fills the left. On the far end of the room is a second sitting area with two doors on the far wall. I make out the end of a bed through one and spot a sink— obviously a bathroom—through the other. Biting my nails for the sole purpose of ensuring my jaw hasn't dropped to my knees, I turn and gawk at the rest of the basement: built-ins, a full-sized pool table, an old-fashioned arcade game, and a bar-height table with chairs in the corner.

"I think this place is bigger than the apartment Mom and I live in."

"My house?" Breckin asks, leaving me standing at the bottom of the steps.

I laugh at the excess laid out before me. "No, your basement."

The fireplace flares to life with the flick of another switch, and Breckin straightens. "Sorry," he says uncomfortably.

My eyes wander the room. No Christmas tree, lights, presents, or stockings. The upstairs was dark and unfestive as well. Christmas is in two weeks. "Don't you celebrate the holidays?"

He's an angel—isn't Christmas a pretty big deal to them?

Breckin's mouth twists, his shoulder sort of popping up in a half shrug as he looks around. He seems indifferent. I should have kept my mouth shut.

"Sorry, that's not my business." I hug myself, and my teeth chatter as a shiver works from my toes to the top of my head.

Breckin grabs a throw. "You're freezing. Take off your shoes and jacket and come sit by the fire."

I wiggle my toes in my boots. They're ice, despite the thick wool socks I wear. The fire looks delectable, but I stand fixed at the base of the stairs—uncertain. Searching my bag, I pull out my phone as Breckin remains beside the fire, his face impassive.

"I won't hurt you."

My eyes lift from my cell.

"You're safe, Vivienne. He won't come here, and I won't hurt you," he repeats.

"I know." I sigh, like I'm surprised the words came from my lips.

Breckin shoves his hair back, his right eye narrowing thoughtfully.

"That sounds ridiculous, doesn't it? After tonight . . . I don't think I truly *know* anything, but . . ." I pause. My fear and hesitation aren't rooted in what he is, or isn't. We've lived in the same town and gone to the same school all our lives. He's got an ego, he causes trouble occasionally, but he's not a bad guy. And he isn't someone I've ever been afraid of. Still, my heart races as nerves dance in my stomach. I'm terrified of letting down my guard. Terrified of my thoughts, my feelings. *Feelings? Where did this come from?*

"I trust you. I'm just—" My shoulders lift when I can't articulate properly.

"Freaked out? Scared as hell? Considering a mental institution?" He says it with such calm—straight-faced, mouth drawn—I can't prevent laughter from bubbling up.

"Well, thank goodness." My fingers fumble with my jacket as my hesitance melts away. "It's nice to know I'm not the only one who thinks I'm crazy."

Breckin's poker face slips as I untangle my bag from around my neck and set it on the floor. I shrug out of my jacket, kick off my boots, and inhale deeply before daring to move forward.

He holds the throw blanket out as I near him and the plump chair he's angled toward the fire. "You're not crazy, Vivienne."

That's debatable. "First things first." Accepting the blanket, I sit and pull my knees to my chest, covering my legs and feet. "I should text Zara so she doesn't call my mom."

"Good idea. Are you hungry? Thirsty?" He crosses the room to the kitchen as I type out a vague text. My gaze flits from the keyboard to his back, unable to not look for evidence of the wings hiding in there somewhere. *Do they hide? Are they magic? Invisible?* "Ask whatever you want."

My head snaps up. Breckin's face reflects in a mirror running from floor to ceiling behind the wet bar. He watches me stare at him. My cheeks burn. Hitting send on my text, I drop the phone to my lap and drag the throw to my chin. The fire works its magic, the flames warming my frozen toes.

"I'm not sure what to ask," I admit, after a moment of watching him watch me.

He pulls two water bottles from a mini refrigerator, his mouth twisting. "You've been watching my backside—"

I choke. "Uh, watching your wings. Not your backside, thank you very much."

"Yes, my wings. That's what I meant, Vivie. I didn't know you had such a dirty mind."

I gape at his smug grin. His tease draws my ire at the same time his calling me Vivie draws goosebumps over my skin. "I do not have a dirty mind."

As if testing me, he twists the lid from his water and drinks half of it—a knowing smile on his perfect face when he's done. Darn my eyes for staring. I face the fire and bite the inside of my cheek.

Breckin sets a bottle of water on the table by my chair and takes a seat on the couch. I peer into the fire, watching the flames leap around the ceramic logs, the blue glow from the gas flickering at the base.

"I like real fires better," I say for no reason, other than to break the silence, my eyes not leaving the fireplace. "There's no snap, crackle, and pop to a gas fire. No faces in the burning logs."

"Faces in the logs?"

"Yeah? Don't you ever stare at the flames? At the way the embers and burnt logs burn into creatures?" My breath catches. Creatures, like demons and dragons—that's what I usually see in a fire. Scary fairytale type things I never considered real, like angels. Now I'm unsure.

"The one upstairs is real. I brought you down here because the lack of windows is safer."

I work up the nerve to face him, to ask my questions. "Safer from what?"

He's sitting on the edge of the couch, his forearms resting on his thighs. He flips his water bottle between his knees and regards me.

"You said you would tell me everything if I came with you. What happened yesterday? Why do I need to be in your basement? Why do I need safety?"

His head falls. "I'm sorry. It's my fault you're in this position."

"Why would this be your fault?"

Yesterday was a normal day. Zara dropped me off after school. I ate a snack with my mom, then changed to go for a run while she got ready for work. She dropped me at my usual trailhead at the base of

Mount Alexa, and I started jogging. For the past three years, I've followed this route—jogging for several miles. Yesterday something happened. Something different.

"You said I was attacked, that you heard me scream. But I have no memory of it. I have no physical injuries." I shake my head, challenging everything he told me.

"You have bruises," he says softly. "On your ribs."

"How would you—"

He sinks into the couch. "Because I took your clothes off, Vivienne. I carried you back to my house and undressed you and made sure you were okay before carrying you home."

My sports bra and running tights. Half my clothing was missing. My shoes were missing. My breathing accelerates, the possibilities filling my mind.

"You were covered in blood. I saw it from the air and . . . it's not the first time I've seen a wild animal attack while out flying, but . . . but I followed the trail. Something drew me down to earth yesterday. Something made me track you."

My fingernails dig into my palms as the blood drains from my face.

"Whatever it was ran off. All I saw was a flash of movement as I came through the trees and saw you lying there."

"No." My feet slip from the chair, dropping to the floor with a thud as I sit forward. "No, that's not right. Blood from where? I'm not injured. I'm fine." A tear slides down my face.

"I'm an angel."

He's no longer cocky and full of egotistical pride. He says those three words as if they're nothing—like reciting the day's weather or answering a simple question. My palm covers my mouth.

It *is* the answer.

He's an angel. He called the other a reaper. *A reaper.*

"You said I was dead. He said you stole me from him." Images flash through my mind. *The rip of claws at my side. The darkness hovering, the pain of a million suns consuming my body, the amber eyes—*

33

Breckin's eyes—filled with worry. My cheeks are hot with tears. "Breckin?"

"You were moments from death. He was here to take your soul. You were supposed to die." His pain-laced voice cuts me deeper than knowing the truth.

But I didn't die. My wounds were healed.

He nods, somehow knowing my thoughts and confirming what I know to be true. "I healed you. I brought you back."

PIECES

BRECKIN

"*A*ngels aren't supposed to interfere in Death's work." I slide to the far end of the couch, putting myself directly across from her. "I won't apologize for it. I couldn't let you die, Viv." Leaning forward, I pluck her hands from her lap.

She's in shock. Her shoulders slumped, her jaw slack, her hands limp in mine. Her eyes seem far away, staring past my face, but I tell her everything. I start at the beginning and explain exactly what I saw when I landed in the snow and found the reaper over her. What he said. How I responded. Finished, I lean closer, my head bobbing around until she meets my gaze.

"I won't let him take you, I swear." My fingers tighten their grasp.

Her face undergoes a kaleidoscope of emotions before she wets her lips and speaks. "On the mountain, earlier . . . he said something."

He said a few things. "Yes?"

"He said you were a son of an angel in love with a human." Her gaze slides left, as her cheeks color. "Is that true?" she asks, returning her ice-blue stare to mine.

"There isn't an easy answer to your question."

"Then the answer is no." She pulls her hands from mine and sits back.

I nearly growl. My hand clutches her blanket-covered knee, because it's the closest thing in my reach, as I lean in, bringing my face inches from hers. "No. The answer isn't that simple."

Our eyes lock and hold in a battle of wills before I remove my hand and give her space. "We barely speak, Vivienne. Would you believe me if I said I was in love with you?"

Her hair dances around her face as she shakes her head. "Of course not."

"But you're angry?"

Her mouth opens, then closes, her head turning to the fire once again as she exhales deeply. If I knew what love was, if I knew how to decipher the emotions she's brought to life in the last twenty-four hours . . . the reaper might be right.

"My mother died giving birth to me, did you know that? My father wasn't around much. I had nannies."

Sadness clouds her eyes. "I remember the nannies."

Sure she does. Kids asked me all the time why I had a 'new mom' every few years. That's what happens when your nannies sleep with your angel father—they don't last long.

"He isn't the easiest, uh . . . person, for lack of a better word. Feelings are weakness. That's what I was raised to believe."

"What do you mean?"

How do I explain the supernatural world to someone who's never known it? "There's a hierarchy amongst angels. Good versus evil. The righteous versus the sinners."

She fidgets in the chair, pulling her legs up. "I know the Bible."

"Then you know angels aren't fat, happy toddlers painted on ceilings. We're warriors, fighters. My father isn't half blood, he's Divine. A Dominion." She works to understand, but her expressive face gives her away. She's lost. My titles and explanations make no sense. Why would they?

"He isn't good." I let my revelation sit for a moment. "And I'm not supposed to be good either."

Unexpectedly, she huffs a light laugh. "What in the world does that mean?"

"I tell you my father is a Dominion angel of sin and you laugh?"

She laughs louder, her fingers going to her lips. Does nothing unnerve her? She's extremely calm, considering she's learned about angels, reapers, and her own near-death experience tonight.

"No, you told me he wasn't good. That is a far cry from . . . what did you call him? A Dominion angel of sin?"

"They're pretty much the same thing. Just different levels of bad, I suppose."

Technicalities. I'm playing a game with words, and Vivienne knows it. Her face twists into the chastising grimace.

"Different levels of bad?" Her shoulders shake with laughter. Her brows knit together, and her smile falters as she inhales sharply. "Is that who the reaper meant, when he said they'd kill you? Was he talking about your father?"

And now she understands the hierarchy of angels. There isn't much loyalty.

"No. My father won't kill me." Not because he loves me as his son. He wants me for what's to come. Rubbing my forehead, I stretch my neck from side to side. "Honestly, I don't know what the reaper meant. I healed you. I interceded where I shouldn't have. There are those who would have a problem with that." *And those who would take issue with me telling her about us to begin with.*

"Are you in trouble?" Her forehead wrinkles as she chews at the edge of a fingernail. "What can they do to you?"

Her concern sparks something within me. The pressure in my chest returns, the talons digging in again. "Of all things, you're worried about me?" I'm astonished.

She snatches a strand of hair and wraps it around her finger. "You saved my life."

I reach for the hair, rubbing it between the pad of my thumb and index finger. "And I'd do it again. I'm not worried about the consequences. The reaper doesn't realize who I am. Who my father is."

Her hand covers mine, dragging it from her hair as she holds my gaze. "What about me?"

What is she asking?

"What happens to me in this whole situation?"

My cell phone buzzes, saving me from replying. I stand and fish it from my pants pocket. It's Elias. I hold a finger up to Vivienne and wander toward the kitchen.

"Hey." I refrain from saying his name to protect his identity. He's been a resident of this town as long as I have. He runs a business, eats, shops, and plays in the same places the rest of us do.

"What the hell did you do tonight? I'm hearing chatter. You know there are eyes everywhere in this town, Breckin."

Damn supernaturals. "The reaper I told you about, he's hanging around and making threats."

"Threatening you?" Elias' voice drips with anger.

"Me. And Vivienne."

Elias growls, and Vivienne's eyes go wide. He'd cause an avalanche if he were up in the mountains.

"Fine. I'll see what I can find out. We shouldn't have a reaper lurking around unless he's doing his job. I was told she saw you both. The Court won't like that. Erase her memory."

"I can't." I turn my back to Vivienne and lower my voice. "It doesn't work on her. I tried last night. Plus, I need her to know everything until I take care of this. I can't keep her safe if she doesn't know."

"It's not your job to keep some human girl safe. You've got bigger decisions to make, Breckin. Your father will be home soon. He'll expect your allegiance."

"I've got four months."

"Breckin," he warns.

"See what you can find out about the reaper and keep Father and the Court away. I'll protect her no matter what, but I could use your help. Please."

"Feeling a bit possessive, are you?"

I look at Vivienne in the mirror. "I'm feeling a whole lot possessive."

"Of course you are. You're an angel, and angels don't like others messing with what belongs to us."

"Thanks, man."

The call ends with Elias promising me a message as soon as he has information. Vivienne stands, and I turn with a shrug. "There's a lot I can't tell you. Things about Havenwood Falls you're not allowed to know."

"There are other angels here?" she asks as she walks across the living room. I nod. "You're protecting them from me?"

"Not exactly, but I suppose in a way, yes. The less you know the better."

"The reaper called you a half-breed like it was a dirty word. Why?"

"Angels weren't created to reproduce with humans. They should have been happy in Paradise, but they weren't. They wanted more. It was forbidden and caused dissent." I rub the back of my neck. "It's really an issue thousands of years in the making."

Her head bobs in understanding. I'd expected more questions.

"What are you feeling possessive over?" she asks, nodding toward my phone as her lips curve seductively. I doubt she knows she's doing it. She's always had this alluring innocence about her.

"I'm two parts of one whole. I'm human, but I'm also angel. My angel side has staked a claim."

She inches forward. "Staked a claim?" Her brow lifts. "On me?"

"It's what the reaper sensed. I don't control my angelic emotions as well as I should. I didn't mask my feelings yesterday, or tonight."

She stops an arm's length away and looks at the floor. "Why did you save me? Would you have stopped for anyone?"

No. I witnessed vampires kill a few months ago. I did nothing. Why was yesterday different? I don't have the answer, but I'd like one. I debate her questions too long. Vivienne clears her throat and crosses her arms.

"You just did, is that it? For no reason?" Her voice trembles. "I don't remember much, but it was quick. Something knocked me down, and there was indescribable pain. That's it. That's all I recall. I should have died. I should have died, but you saved me, and now here I am."

I cave, the human and the angel. Her emotions, her fear—it's too much for me. Snatching her by the waist, I pull her into my arms. "It wasn't for no reason. There's something about you. I should have flown right on by, but something hooked me." My nose burns with the memory. The smell was foreign. "The scent of your blood, something . . . it called to me. I didn't have a choice."

I shake my head, frustrated at having so many questions, and so few answers. Vivienne grimaces. "Is there something wrong with my blood?"

The answer to that would open a whole new can of worms. One issue at a time.

"There's nothing wrong with you or your blood. I'm sorry. I know this is a lot to take in. Trust me, I'm afraid I killed you by saving your life. I thought I could erase your memory, and everything would go back to normal. I didn't expect a psycho reaper or these feelings."

Her eyes light up. "I thought feelings were a weakness?"

"As a human, they are. They make you soft. As an angel, though . . . the angel is smarter than the human. He's enamored with you. I can't do anything about that, and I will protect what's mine, Vivie."

She leans into me, her hands settling on my hips. "So you *are* staking a claim."

"How does that make you feel?"

She glances down, before raising her eyes to mine. "I like it when you call me Vivie."

Her body against mine ignites desire, and I curl my fingers into her sweater as my wings beg for release. "Do you?"

She nods with a smirk. My head lowers; my lips find hers, brushing a quick kiss before drawing back.

Vivienne's hands slip up my chest, wrapping around my neck and tugging me back. Her lips toy with mine, pressing small kisses back and forth over and over but never drawing me in. My pulse accelerates, and fire ignites in my veins, spreading quickly. Vivienne yelps as I pick her up and plop her on the kitchen counter behind us.

She leans back when I move to kiss her again. "Angel strength?"

"That, and you're five foot nothing." I wink and move between her knees, happy she's somewhat level with me.

"We can't all be perfectly built angels."

I'm perfectly built? I study her. The delicate, heart-shaped face, her pouting lips, her silky hair, the graceful ballerina limbs on her petite frame. Anyone with a sinister mind could snap her in two without breaking a sweat. I brush my knuckles across her cheek, my fingers sliding into her hair and moving it from her face. "Everything about you is perfect. Too perfect for me."

We meet halfway. Her mouth opens, allowing me a small taste. I mold my lips to hers, and her socked feet hook around my thighs, drawing me closer.

"What is happening between us, Breck?" she asks as her fingers lose themselves in my hair. "What is this?"

There's so much confusion written on her face. I feel it, too.

"I don't know."

It's the most honest thing I can say. A switch flipped last night when I healed her. No, before I healed her. Things changed when I heard her scream. I know plenty of shifters. I'm aware of how they find mates. Angels don't have mates, we don't imprint, but I swear to the maker, this girl imprinted on me. On all of me—the divine side, as well as my soul.

DEMONS AT THE DOOR

VIVIENNE

I toss and flip to my stomach, hiding my head beneath a pillow as thumping bass rattles my headboard. Why do the neighbors insist on blaring their music on the weekends?

Three raps at my door wake me further. "What?" I whine, my feet flailing like a kid having a temper tantrum.

"Hey, sleepyhead, you getting up?" Mom pops her head in.

"Sleepyhead?" I roll to my back, and my eyes focus on Mom's jeans and sweater. "What time is it?" She typically sleeps until after lunch when she works nights. Why is she up this early? Even her blond hair is fixed in a no-fuss braid, instead of her usual work ponytail.

"It's after noon. I thought we could go to lunch and do a little shopping today."

After noon? I push up from the bed, and a wave of nausea hits me.

"I can't believe you're still sleeping. You're usually the one waking me on Sundays. Did you and Zara stay out all night partying?" She steps farther into the room, no real accusation in her words. She knows us better than that, but . . . I clutch my stomach.

"Viv?" She's across the room and pushing back my hair, the back of her hand on my forehead before I can blink. "Are you not feeling well?" She turns my face to hers. "You're pale, but not feverish. You look tired."

"I must have picked up a bug at school. I'm okay, just a little green."

She leans in, her light eyes searching. "Well, shoot. We need to Christmas shop."

"You go then. I can take care of myself." Fear settles around me. I pull a pillow to my chest.

"I'll shop tomorrow. How about I make my famous grilled cheeses and we find a good movie to watch?" She pats my knee as I nod. "I'll start lunch."

She crosses my room, grabbing a dirty cup from my dresser before turning. "You must have been tired to fall asleep in your clothes. You haven't done that since you were six," she says with a smile, pulling the door closed behind her.

My head spins, and I grab my hair to keep it in place. *My clothes?* I'm wearing jeans and a sweater. I bolt for my bathroom and lose the meager contents of my stomach.

We spend the afternoon watching movies on the couch. This is a normal Sunday for us, but everything feels wrong. I check my phone, re-reading the text I sent Zara last night:

Decided against going to the clinic. Went home instead, feeling okay but tired. Enjoy movie night and I'll see you Monday.

I recall the Burger Bar. I have a vague memory of snow and being cold. A flash of fire—and nothing else. No memory of texting Zara. No memory of coming home. Mom laughs at a scene in our third romantic comedy, and I tuck my legs closer. My chest is empty, like something is missing. I close my eyes as they burn with tears. Whether from my raging headache or because of the gaping hole, I can't be sure. *What is going on with me?*

By the time Zara arrives outside my apartment building Monday morning, I've run through every scenario imaginable. Maybe someone slipped drugs into my food Saturday night? Maybe I'm crazy. Maybe I've been sucked into some alternate universe, like in the last book I read.

"Your carriage, my lady," Zara shouts through the open passenger side window as I lock the apartment and hurry to the car.

I toss my backpack over the seat and jump in. "You're letting all the heat out."

"Feeling better?" she asks as I buckle my seatbelt and get situated.

I consider confiding in her, then swiftly change my mind. *What would I say?* I keep seeing her standing beside me outside my apartment window, calling me paranoid. *When was that?* It must be recent, and yet I can't recall. *Nope. I can't tell her.*

"All better." I switch the air vents to warm my gloved hands and change the subject. "Tell me about the movies."

Zara gasps as she shifts into drive. "Girl. I finally confirmed it with my own two eyes. Graysin Ravenal and Everett Weston are dating."

"I thought we'd already confirmed that."

"It was rumor. Now we can mark it down as fact. They are so freaking gorgeous together. I kind of hate her. I want an Everett of my own."

"Z, he's gotta be pushing thirty."

"Twenty-eight," she corrects. "I think I need an older man. I'm sick of the boys we have to pick from at school. They're ridiculous. Saturday night—" I bend over, re-tying the laces on my boots as Zara complains. "—then a bunch of the guys from the football team started shoving each other and screwing around. I swear, they act like wild animals. How they get dates is beyond me."

"They're all tall, dark, and gorgeous." Tossing my hair, I sit up and look out the front windshield.

Zara sighs. "Ain't that the truth."

I should remind her how she sat on the knee of one of those football players, flirting wildly during lunch Friday. My mouth opens to do just that when a dark figure captures my attention. We're stopped at the light at Eighth and Main, and he's leaning against the side of Pyntz Butcher Shoppe looking like sin—all pale skin, jet black hair, and dark clothing.

"Z, do you see him?" I grab Zara's forearm, my gaze fixated on the guy. "Across the street."

"Who? Mr. Emo?" The light changes, and we pull forward. "Isn't that the guy from Saturday?" She squints as we turn onto Main with the traffic and pass a sidewalk width from him.

From Saturday? Vibrant blue eyes flash, and my stomach drops. Too afraid to turn in my seat, I check the side mirror. Sweat peppers my forehead as he watches us drive away. My body goes cold.

"He's creepy." I force my eyes to stop looking.

Zara pshaws. "Creepy? I thought you two were going to need a room after the way you stared each other down the other night. Then he disappeared and you left—" Zara inhales sharply, slapping her palm against the steering wheel. "You liar! You didn't get sick, did you? You left with him."

"What? No. Are you kidding? I don't even know him." I twist, looking for the stranger over my shoulder. It's cold and not yet eight in the morning, making him easy to spot on the mostly vacant sidewalk.

"Well, he must be stalking you then, because that's the guy from the other night. You should totally talk to him next time you see him. He's hot." Zara's finger jabs my side as I watch the object of our conversation.

He walks quickly—too quickly. I do a double-take, surprised at how close he is. He removes his hand from the pocket of his long black coat, and my head fills with visions of him pulling a gun and shooting, like some gangster. Instead he lifts his hand to chest level and moves it from left to right. Strange, but nothing like a shootout.

Chiding my ridiculous imagination, I turn back to the front. "Z, I think I'm—"

"Watch out!" Zara screams. Her hands grip the steering wheel as the car jerks and skids along the ice-painted road.

Car horns blare, my seatbelt locks across my chest, and someone shouts, as a city tour bus stops, sideways, five feet from my door.

"You girls okay?" a voice asks, followed by tapping on the window.

Words fail me. My body shakes. Zara's curses fill the car, as do her thanks. "Vivienne? Zara?"

At the sound of my name, I look up and find Mr. Zander from school jiggling the handle to my door, his face concerned. My hand reaches forward and unlocks the car door, pushing as he pulls it open.

We're an hour late for school by the time Sheriff Kasun finishes with us. No one was hurt, nothing damaged.

"I swear, Viv. Our light was green. The bus driver wasn't paying attention." Zara yanks the school door open, the heat welcoming after standing outside.

"We're fine. I'm not mad." I check my watch. "Let's hurry and get excuse slips. The bell's about to ring."

"You're not mad, but I am. He could have killed you," she says, her face still devoid of color as we walk toward the administration office. "How are you so calm? That bus barreling toward us won't stop flashing through my mind. That's my second near miss this semester! I'll have nightmares for weeks, and you probably want to stop riding with me."

I stop walking and push her to the edge of the hallway. "Look at me." She does, and her eyes glisten with unshed tears. "That thing with Willa was all on her. Not your fault. Neither was this. We're both safe. We're safe, Z," I repeat, hugging her as the class bell sounds. "Come on."

We secure tardy slips from the office and head separate ways. I duck my head and attempt maneuvering the crowded halls of Havenwood Falls High without being stopped. A few students drove around our near-wreck this morning, their faces gawking like typical rubberneckers, which meant the whole school was aware before first period. Not in the mood for discussion, I slip into chemistry instead of hanging in the hall as I normally would. Three other students are already in their seats as I walk down my aisle.

Electricity shocks my wrist, and I gasp, twisting to find my arm in Breckin Roberts' grip. My pulse accelerates.

"Sorry." Breckin removes his hand, balling his fingers into a fist as he leans back and looks up at me. I stare as undecipherable whispers nag at the back of my mind. "Rumor has it you and Zara Shannon almost collided with a bus this morning. You okay?"

There's an edge to his voice as his eyes search me from head to toe like he's checking for injuries.

"I'm fine, thanks." I drop my backpack to the floor and lower into my chair. *What was that?* Breckin and I have barely spoken since elementary school. He defended me from a few jerks in town freshman year, but other than that . . . The sensation of being watched crawls up my spine. The knowledge that Breckin's eyes are fastened on my back sends me scooching down until my neck presses against the back of the chair and my butt hangs over the seat edge. *Thank goodness I'm short.*

I close my eyes and replay everything from this morning. Those blue eyes penetrate the thick layers of fog surrounding my mind. *I know him. I do, but how?*

More students walk into class, their laughter and conversations making me an outsider. A few people say hi. I offer vague smiles as the seats around me fill up.

"Hey, Viv. I saw Zara in the hallway. You two must have had a guardian angel watching over you this morning, huh?" Zal Purser asks as she tugs on the turquoise beads around her neck.

I half fall out of my desk, my heart rate accelerating as I lurch into a sitting position. "What did you say?" I ask, my voice unfamiliar to my own ears.

"I said you must have a guardian angel looking out for you."

Angel. My head whips toward Breckin. He's watching, his amber eyes narrow, his jaw tight. *Guardian angel. Blue eyes. Angel, angel, angel . . .*

Dark spots fill my vision. I sway in my seat, grasping at the edge of my desk, when a hard body presses against my shoulder and arms wrap around me.

Heat blows around my cheek. "Vivie?"

Vivie. The lock unlatches, and memories rush in. The animal attack, the reaper, the bathroom at Burger Bar, Breckin's kisses. I suck shallow breaths, recalling the danger, the warnings. The way the reaper waved a hand this morning and how a bus almost killed me.

"Breck!" I turn into his chest and grab his shirt. "It was him. The bus, this morning . . . I know it was."

Then I see his hands at my waist as he lifts me onto a counter at his house and his smile as his lips descend on mine. My gasp is audible. *Saturday night. He erased my memory?*

Someone calls our teacher as Breckin rubs my arms and helps me stand, supporting most of my weight.

"Vivienne?" Heels click against the floor as she nears.

"I'll take her to the office. She's still freaked out about this morning," Breckin offers, his voice take-charge and firm.

Breckin grabs my bag and escorts me from class. My eyes focus straight ahead, ignoring the curious glances, especially from friends. They're probably wondering when Breckin Roberts and I became close enough for me to cling to him as though my life depends on it.

The hall is empty, the bell having already rung, but neither of us speaks as he ushers me down the corridor and around a corner, where he opens a door and pulls me inside. We're in a janitor's closet, the scent of bleach and bathroom soap overwhelming.

His back to me, he rubs his neck with an exhale as he leans forward and rests his forehead against the door. His hunter green thermal clings to his shoulders and back, and I stare, searching for the wings I now remember. He twists around, remaining against the door, his mouth tight as he shoves his hands into his pockets.

"Why?"

"Are you okay?"

I snort at his insane question. "Am I okay? Where should I start?" Breckin's mouth opens, and I forge ahead. "We kissed. I thought it meant something, but you erased my memory—"

"Vivie?"

I look past the tenderness in his eyes and continue. "I mean, I suppose that's no different than not getting a call back after a date, right? If you were human, I guess that's what this would be—a one-time, never speak to me again hookup. One could argue you were doing me a favor. Taking away my memories is nicer than letting me linger over what happened."

"That's not what happened." Anger flashes across his face as he steps away from the door.

I move, kicking a mop bucket of dirty water. "No? How often do you do this anyway? No wonder I've never heard tales of you with girls. Do you erase every idiot's mind once you have a taste?"

His snarl, purely angelic, scares the hair straight up on my neck. "Vivienne." He grabs my arms, and my back bumps into the shelves stocked with toilet paper and paper towels. Two rolls fall to the floor as Breckin presses close. "You are *not* an idiot, and I didn't erase your memories. Didn't you hear me Saturday night when I told you I was staking my claim? Yesterday was hell for me. And this morning—" His hands move to my face, holding me tight as his forehead touches mine. "When I heard about the accident, it took all my strength to stay away. I figured it would seem odd if I showed up."

My hurt evaporates with his words. I grip his wrists. "I'm not supposed to remember you, am I?"

"You're not." Although his voice is serious, his lips tug into a smile.

"Who erased my memory, Breck?"

His mouth opens, then closes as he chooses his words. "Another angel."

"The one you spoke to the other night?" He nods. "Why?"

"Because if we're not careful, this will become about more than a reaper."

MY IMMORTAL

BRECKIN

*U*ncertainty clouds Vivienne's eyes as my words sink in. This is insane. I'm torn by the return of her memories. I want to take her mouth right here in this closet and drink her in until kissing her erases the fear that buried me this morning when I heard about the accident. At the same time, I want to rage at my angelic abilities until I figure out why they don't work on her. Why does she remember?

Her exhale teases across my face as her hands wrap around my waist. "I don't want to forget, Breck."

The panic in her blue eyes infuriates my protective side. My hand slips around her neck and tucks her head under my chin. "We're trying to keep you safe."

"From the reaper?"

"Among other things," I say vaguely. "And his name is Sebastian, by the way."

She pulls back. "He has a name? How do you know it?"

Might as well tell her what I know, but not here. Not now. I brush her hair back with a smile. "I'd rather not have this conversation in a janitor's closet at school."

"After school, then? Will you tell me everything?"

Everything I can, I say in my head as I nod.

THE DAY DRAGS, and not seeing Vivienne after we part doesn't help. Her messages do, though. She texts me little tidbits about each of her classes, which keeps my brain from exploding with worry until, at last, the day ends.

She blew off my request to meet at her locker, saying she knew where I parked. It bruised my ego, her not wanting me to wait for her. So here I am, leaning against my Bronco and waiting, somewhat impatiently, for her to come to me. The moment her voice cuts across the noise and reaches me, my muscles relax. Cars, music, and hundreds of students crowd out of the building, yet her voice stands out among them all. My soul breathes a sigh of relief. She's surrounded by friends, a warm interested smile on her face as she listens to Macy Blackstone talk about her weekend. Macy's a witch hunter. How would Vivienne react if she knew? What would she think if she knew about the shifters, vampires, and mages who control much of this town? There's so much she doesn't know, so much I can't tell her.

Macy leaves with a wave, and Vivienne scans the lot. A spark ignites within, like the flick of a match, when her blue eyes find me. This girl consumes me. My soul tugs like it would rip itself from my body to reach her side.

My soul?

Vivienne toys with a strand of hair, twirling it as she smiles and nods at her friends, while her eyes remain locked on mine. I straighten and move around the hood. I need her to come over here. Now.

At my movement, she steps down from the curb. "I better go," she says over her shoulder.

"You're not riding home with Zara?" asks Scarlet.

Vivienne hesitates, her steps slowing as mine quicken. Spinning her back to me, she answers, "No. I'm . . . um, I've got another ride today."

I catch the confused look on their faces. Vivienne rides with Zara every day. We don't have to be friends for me to know this. It's a small school, a small town. Everyone knows. The same way everyone knows

Zara drops her off, then heads to Napoli's, where she does her homework, eats, then works the dinner shift until ten.

Gazes shift between Vivienne and me. "With who?"

"Me," I answer for her.

Vivienne twirls, finding me standing in front of her. I don't watch her friends, but I imagine their faces are about as stunned as Vivienne's.

"Hey," she says breathlessly, her lips curving into a deliciously shy smile.

"Hey, yourself." I draw her backpack from her shoulder and swing it onto mine. "You ready?"

Her face flushes as I slip her hand into mine.

"They're staring, aren't they?" Vivienne asks when I look back.

"They're not the only ones." Half the departing students track us by the time I open the passenger door.

Vivienne's hand goes to her hair, twirling again as she tugs the other from my grip. "Great. What are we going to tell people?"

I toy with the zipper on her jacket, my need to be close growing by the second. "Tell them we're going out."

Vivienne's head falls back, her shout of laughter taking me by surprise. Inside, my soul growls, ordering my hand to take hers again. It's damn needy today.

She makes a face. "Like they'll believe that."

She's right, though not because people wouldn't believe I'm attracted to her. She's beyond beautiful. She has plenty of admirers, but I've never been on that list. I've never been one to single out any girl. I go to parties, hang out, and flirt, but holding hands and making a public declaration? I've never done that.

My fingers curl around her wrist, pulling her hand from her hair and using it to draw her closer. Her lips part, and I take advantage, capturing them in a quick kiss.

"Now they will," I say as I pull away. I look around. Sure enough, we've made a scene.

"No," Vivienne whispers as her fingers take my chin and bring my attention back. She slides her hand down around my neck, applying pressure and drawing me to her mouth. "Let's be sure they get the picture."

Her words awaken the need I have for her. Her scent—the deeper underlying scent of her soul—fills my head, and I'm drunk on her. She tempts my human soul and fires up the angel within. She wants me as much as I want her. Whatever this is between us, it is not one-sided. We're so connected, I meet her lips move for move. She shifts right; I shift left. She sucks my bottom lip; I tighten my grip and bite hers. We're lost in each other, in the middle of the school parking lot.

"I think that'll do it." I chuckle at the gawkers pointing and whispering, when we manage to separate. Vivienne releases a giggle in her throat and heaven help me, my desire builds again. Swallowing hard, I move from the open car door. "Let's go to my house."

With an apologetic grin on her face, she waves to her friends as I close her door. Once I'm in the vehicle and buckled, I turn in my seat. "I'm sorry if that was out of line."

Vivienne's face scrunches. "Kissing me?"

"Yeah. In front of your friends and all. I couldn't help myself."

She bites her lip, her eyes flicking to her lap. "I know the feeling. The moment I spotted you, I had this ridiculous desire to run across the parking lot. Is there something about your angelic heritage that lures women in?"

My hand slides across the seat and finds hers. "Have I lured you in?"

"That would be crazy, right? I can't be falling for you, Breck, I know nothing about you."

"You *know* the most important thing about me," I counter, interlacing our fingers.

She scowls, although it's ruined by the smirk that follows immediately after. "I meant, the things couples share when they're falling in love. Your favorite foods, movies, music. The normal things."

It's my turn to scowl. I shake free from her hand and start the car. "Right. 'Cause being part angel is definitely not normal."

Shifting into gear, I grip the steering wheel as an odd mix of emotions flows through me. *She isn't rejecting me. She kissed the hell out of me two minutes ago, for everyone to see. So why am I let down by her comments on love? Why the hell am I acting like a girl? Get your crap together, Breckin.*

"No," she says after a long moment of silence. "Being angel is not normal, but neither is falling for one."

"But, you just said—"

"I'm falling for you, Breck. It's not reasonable, and it makes no sense, but I know it like I know my own name. I know it here." She taps her chest.

Her soul.

With my foot firmly on the brake, I lean across the cab and kiss her hard. "Vivie," I say against her lips, my hand gripping the back of her head. "I feel it, too."

Her hand touches my cheek as she pulls away. "That's why the reaper wants me, isn't it?"

I still.

"He sensed your feelings, he said he would take my soul away from you, he told me not to let you taint it."

She's right.

Our bond is through our souls. *Soul mates.* It makes perfect sense.

And it's exactly the type of thing that would drive a reaper crazy with power.

I hold her gaze. "It doesn't matter what he wants. He's not getting it."

"You sound so confident."

"I'm an angel, Vivie." She cracks a smile. It's small, but it's there, and it lights up the dark corners of my being, and breathes life into me. She's changing me with every look, touch, and smile. I'm hers. "Tell me about this morning."

My hand holds hers all the way home as she explains what happened with Zara and the reaper, Sebastian.

"And you're sure it was him? You said you had no memories before you saw me in chemistry." I turn onto Fairchild and pull directly into our drive, waiting as the garage door opens.

"I'm certain. When I saw him, I had this immediate reaction. I didn't have to know why I knew him, there was just something off. Something that made me wary. And after—" She doesn't finish. She shakes, like she's working a shiver through her body.

We pull into the garage, and I cut the engine. I pump her hand in mine as she reaches for the door. "Wait. Stay there."

Hurrying around the Bronco, I make sure the garage door closes all the way before opening her door and extending my hand.

"You're a gentleman? Who knew?" She teases as she jumps down from the jacked-up seat with an "umph."

"I'll find you a stool."

Her fist connects with my abs, then flattens, rubbing where the punch landed when I grunt. "Oh, sorry. I didn't mean to hit you so hard."

"Aw, you're cute, tiny girl. You think your little baby punch hurt me?"

Her palms slap at my stomach, pushing, as she walks around me. "You know there is such a thing as being too cocky."

"Not for an angel." I wrap her in a bear hug from behind, inhaling her scent. *Intoxicating.* She melts into me, her back molding with my chest until we're one.

She sighs and hooks her hands around my forearms. "I'm scared."

"I know you are." As if I can infuse her with my courage, I squeeze tighter. "I won't let anything happen to you. He can't kill you, it's against the rules." Then again, he isn't playing by the rules anymore.

She turns, her eyes skeptical. "What about today?"

"He wanted to scare you. Or me. Sebastian is playing a dangerous game." *One that will end with him ceasing to exist if he threatens Vivienne again.*

"This is too much. I don't think I can deal with this. Maybe I don't want my memories, maybe I—"

"It's too late." I clasp her to my chest. "Memories or not, he knows who you are and *what* you are to me. He's not going to stop."

"So what do we do?"

Hunt Sebastian down and end him. Vivienne's fear prevents me from saying the words. "We go inside. We take an hour to eat and think about anything other than Sebastian. Then, we call my uncle."

I head for the door, but her hand yanks me back when she doesn't follow. "Breck?" Her fingers tighten around my hand. "What am I to you?"

My eyes scan the frailty of her. This delicately beautiful slip of a girl who claimed my soul and is taking possession of my heart.

"My soul mate."

SOMEONE TO YOU

VIVIENNE

"*Y*ou have an uncle?"

I follow Breckin into the house, and this time we stay on the main floor. He points to the stools sitting at the kitchen counter, telling me to have a seat as he raids the refrigerator. *Seriously?* He throws words like soul mate around, then drags me into his million-dollar kitchen and offers me a snack? *How did this become my life?*

Soul mate. My mind refuses to process his words. I'm numb.

"Sort of. We're not related, but he's the closest thing I have to family."

"Is he the one who erased my memories Saturday night?"

A jar of nacho cheese slides across the pristine marble counter as he shuts the refrigerator. "Yeah." He moves to a pantry the size of my bedroom and grabs a bag of chips.

"And what does he think of all this?" I prod, when he doesn't elaborate.

"Chip?" He pops the lid from the jar, dipping a blue corn chip into the sauce.

"Breck?"

"Vivie?" His brow arches. I force back a reply at his flippant tone.

"What does your uncle think of this?" I wave a hand between us.

"You can ask him when he arrives." He stretches across the counter and holds a chip out. "Eat."

"Did you just order me to eat?" I bristle, taking the chip without thought.

"Order is a strong word." He dips another. "I asked."

I cross my legs and square my shoulders, taking a breath. "You most certainly did not ask."

The corner of his mouth tugs up. "Are you mad at me for trying to make you eat something?"

The chip he handed me drops to the counter, the glob of fake cheese smearing yellow across the gorgeous white. "I'm mad at you for ignoring my questions and yes, for trying to make me eat."

"You're not hungry?"

"Oh my gosh. That is not the point, Breckin."

My flustered outburst is met with a flirtatious grin. It takes all my willpower to remain across the four-foot kitchen island from him. *This boy makes me crazy.*

Exasperated, I lean back. "Do you always get what you want?"

"Yes." There's no shame in his answer. I clamp my jaw.

My weak soul dances at his cockiness as my independent mind theorizes ways to knock him off his high horse. As though he knows exactly what I'm thinking, he smiles and tilts his head, his amber-flecked eyes pinning me to my seat. His intense gaze sends heat creeping up my neck. I wipe my palms on my thighs as Breckin's entire face transforms. A tight mask of concentration takes over as he straightens his back and breathes with precision—his chest rising and falling slowly.

Something teases across my mind, and I jerk back, gasping for air.

Breckin blinks, his face relaxing as a small scowl appears.

I grip the counter and watch him closely as the feeling withdraws. "What did you just do?"

His scowl deepens.

"What did you do, Breckin?" My stool clatters back as I stand. Fists form at my sides.

Breckin wipes at his forehead with a curse. "I'm sorry."

He hurries around the counter, and I step back, unnerved by his actions. His face falls.

"Vivie?" Breckin lifts his hands in a silent plea for forgiveness. "I'm sorry. I shouldn't have. I was trying to use compulsion. I never—"

"Compulsion? To make me eat?" I spit the words at him.

"You argued with me."

That's his excuse? "I'm sorry? I argued with you?"

"No, that's not what I meant. I mean, it is, but—" He scratches his head. "I wanted you to eat. You were arguing, and it made me wonder if I could—"

"Oh. My." Swallowing, I groan and walk away, needing space. Halfway across the kitchen, I turn back. "You arrogant angel. You think you can order me to eat and sit and stay. That I won't ask questions? Do you want me to blush and giggle while following you around like the other girls do?"

Breckin's shoulders shake as his lips quirk.

"Are you *laughing* at me?" I ask, the urge to punch him strong.

His face goes blank.

"Don't ever try it again, Breckin," I order, nearly stomping my foot.

"I won't. I promise. I would never try to control you, Vivie. I was curious if it were possible. Since erasing your mind didn't work."

"I mean it, never again. It's horrible. Like spiders crawling around in my mind. Sebastian did it, too. I hate it."

Breckin stiffens. "Sebastian was in your head? When?"

His tone kills my anger. "Saturday night. I don't know if he was *in* my head, but it felt the same."

He pulls his cell from his pocket, holding up a finger when I ask what he's doing. Tugging on my sleeves, I fold my arms across my chest and wait.

"We need you." His eyes stay on mine as he nods. "Nope. She remembers everything." There's a pause as he listens to the person on the other end of the line. "Okay. Yeah." After a few vague, one-word answers, the call ends, and he sets his cell on the counter. "Can you stay for dinner?"

"If I say no, will you try to force me?"

He blows out his cheeks. "No, Viv. I'll never try to compel you again."

"Damn straight you won't." Breckin cracks a smile. "Of course I'll stay. He's coming?"

"He is, in about two hours."

My pulse kicks up a notch, my nerves fluttering to life. Breckin pushes the stool I kicked back to the counter and comes toward me. His hand touches the bottom edge of my sweater, tugging it. I take a step toward him as he takes another toward me.

"I'm truly sorry." His hand brushes my cheek as it wraps around my head. "I know this is a horrible excuse, but . . . everything feels different with you. It's new territory. My curiosity got the best of me."

I hook a finger through his belt loop and pull us closer still.

"Different how?" My voice is husky and broken. My soul, or whatever it is within me that seems to want him, flutters.

"I've compelled humans before, to forget what they saw, or to get what I want." I frown, and he grimaces. "It's easy with them. A touch or a look and a thought, and they do what I need. You don't work that way. My abilities don't work on you at all. It's . . ."

"Freaking you out? Scaring you? Making you consider a mental institution?" I repeat his own words.

"Frustrating as hell," he says with a short laugh. "And all of those other things. Hopefully, Elias will have answers."

"Elias?" There's one Elias in town that I know of. Elias Jamison, the owner of Havenwood Falls Ski-Ventures. Besides transporting thrill seekers up the mountains on ski runs, he does life-flights for the clinic. Mom has spoken of him a few times, but I rarely see him around town. *He's an angel?*

"I can tell by your face you're making the connection, and I'm sure you have questions, but I have a favor to ask." *Questions? Only about a million of them. Elias Jamison is an angel.* I've never felt anything strange around him. I've never . . . unless my memories have been wiped before.

"Vivie." Breckin's finger tilts my chin. "You're thinking way too hard."

Counting to three, I inhale and release a deep breath. Breckin grins.

"Can we just chill for a bit? Have a snack and talk until he gets here? About normal things?" Breckin asks, with hope in his voice.

"About normal things?"

"Yeah. Like your favorite food, movies, and music. You know, the stuff people learn when they're falling in love with each other."

I stretch up on my toes. "I think I heard that somewhere before."

Even at my tallest, my lips are nowhere near his. He presses a kiss to my forehead, understanding my hint. Well, somewhat understanding, since I wanted his lips on mine. Mildly placated, I drop to the flats of my feet. I must frown, because Breckin chuckles and hauls me into his body, his arms solid against my back as he lowers his head.

"I know your soul. I want to know the rest of you, Vivie. I want to know everything."

The anticipation sends giddy sparks through my body. "Everything? That might take a while."

Two inches from my lips, he pauses. "Then let's start with the important things."

I wet my lips. My body is a firecracker waiting for the fuse to reach the explosives. Everything tenses as a smile forms. "Easy. I'm wildly attracted, and attached, to an angel."

A deep growl fills his chest, rumbling through his entire body as his eyes darken and arms tighten.

"Would you kiss me already?" I half ask, half order.

The explosives ignite.

WE'VE MOVED to the basement, Breckin preferring the safety of being underground to the open windows of the main floor, when Elias arrives.

"He brought pizza." Breckin smiles, giving my leg a tender squeeze before leaving me on the couch and moving to the kitchen. I rest my arms on the back of the couch, my gaze following him. "Enhanced smell," he says at my dubious stare.

Enhanced smell, senses, vision, and hearing. He's my own superhero. I track the noises above. It's obvious from the way Elias parked in the garage and entered the house on his own that he is considered family. When his heavy steps hit the wood of the staircase, I stand and straighten my hair and sweater.

Breckin sends me a wink, I take a breath, the stairs creak, and then Elias appears.

Elias Jamison is what most would picture when thinking about a Colorado mountain man. He's stout and burly. Half a foot shorter than Breckin's six-two, he's got the shape of a bodybuilder and the dark, wiry beard of an outdoorsman. He plops the boxes in his hand onto the counter and turns my way.

"Vivienne," he says, with the type of gravelly voice rock stars envy. His bright blue eyes look me up and down.

I open my mouth, but did words come out? I try again. "I don't remember you from Saturday. You were here, right? You erased my memory." It's not hello, but the questions have built up.

His full mouth cracks a smile. "Breckin told me you were a curious one."

My gaze shifts to Breckin, who lifts his brows as if daring me to deny it.

"Well, you know. It's not every day a girl comes under attack from reapers and falls for an angel." I attempt a nonchalant shrug, but Elias's black look freezes the humor on my lips.

"Falls for?" He glares at Breckin.

Oh. Oh, crap. I should have kept that to myself. It popped out, my lovesick heart and soul not seeing anything wrong with how I feel. Sebastian's warning hits me. *A son of angels in love with a human? They will kill you once they find out.*

"It's not his fault." I hurry to the end of the counter, putting myself between them. "We're not in love or anything. He's—"

"Viv." Breckin grabs my shoulder and pulls me into his side. "It's fine. He wouldn't hurt me. Or you."

Elias's gaze volleys between us, his face thoughtful. After a moment of tense silence, he wipes a hand across his face and through his hair, lifting his baseball cap, then replacing it before he finally releases a long exhale.

"Soul mates."

Hearing the word from Elias's mouth is confirmation. Breckin squeezes my shoulder.

"How do you know?" I ask, when neither of them speak.

"His pull toward you Friday night. The fact that neither of us could erase him from your memories. The look in his face. And yours." Elias huffs a light laugh. "I've seen many teenage girls wear the same head-over-heels-in-love look, Vivienne. I've never seen it on Breckin."

I have a head-over-heels-in-love look on my face? My cheeks warm. *He does?* I can't help but glance up at Breckin.

"You're right," Breckin says, smiling down at me. "She's totally falling head over heels in love with me."

I punch him.

KNOCKING ON HEAVEN'S DOOR

BRECKIN

*W*e sit around the fire, our pizza—from Napoli's, Viv's favorite—on the coffee table before us, and take turns filling Elias in on every detail of the past seventy-two hours. Vivienne describes her feelings in such detail, I find myself taking her hand in mine on more than one occasion. The fear she felt when she woke Friday night after I left her. The not knowing what happened but feeling so off.

"It made me feel sick, Elias. Whatever it is you did when you wiped my mind. Don't do it again," Vivienne says, chiding him like a parent.

"That would be the soul mate connection." Vivienne's brow lifts, and Elias clarifies. "It is extremely powerful. Most consider it a gift given by the maker to fulfill the order of things."

Vivienne's eyes grow as they flit between us, her mouth gaping.

"In human terms, it means we were matched to fulfill our destiny," I provide helpfully.

Or not so helpfully, judging by the way her stunned face swings my way.

"Destiny?"

"C'mon, Viv. Don't tell me you don't believe in destiny? That people are put in places to make things happen, or sometimes bad things happen to good people because they need to learn a lesson that will bring them to something better?"

"I think you've been scrolling the internet for motivational memes," Vivienne says. Elias clears his throat, cutting off a low chuckle. She shrugs at him before returning her attention to me. "I don't know what I believe in. Maybe things happen for a reason. Maybe it's coincidence."

I face her on the couch and take her hands. "We're not a coincidence, Vivie."

Elias' face sobers as he sits forward and speaks. "A soul mate is forever, Vivienne. No one can take him from you or you from him. That is why you felt sick when we tried to wipe your memory. Your soul fought for what your mind forgot."

She releases a sigh. "Why? What purpose is there in giving Breckin me as a soul mate?"

Her mouth turns, a small pout forming. I cup her face in my hands. "Hey. Are you kidding me? You and your beautiful soul, and all the amazing things you do? I remember the campaign you started in third grade for the buddies bench on the playground after that new kid cried because she didn't have any friends, and you were so upset because you didn't know she was alone. Or what about all of your volunteer work? The food drives in town square, the tutoring you do?"

Her eyes glisten. "How do you know about those things?"

The truth hits me. "The real question is how did I ignore what's between us for so long? I've watched you for years. I've watched you, and I hoped that one day you'd look at me and give me the time of day. Sebastian was right about you being special. I'm the one who doesn't deserve you."

Leaning forward, she kisses my cheek and hugs me. "You have to say that. Your soul is connected to mine."

"Yes, because it was made for me," I say, hugging her quickly, then pulling back and looking in her eyes. "Whatever the reason, Vivienne, we were put together, and we will remain together."

"I still say you got the short end of the stick." She pats my cheek playfully as she stands and bends close to my ear. "I won myself a hot supernatural who can fly me all over the world. You got a tiny human who can't drive and sings off-key." She winks.

Elias regards her with a touch of amusement and a whole lot of admiration as she excuses herself. He waits until the bathroom door closes before speaking his mind.

"This is dangerous, Breckin. You know that, right?"

I drop the confidence I've held all afternoon. The moment I put it all together, the moment I knew we were soul mates, I realized we were screwed.

"What am I supposed to do? We can't erase her memories of me. I can't compel her. I tried—it did not go well. Is it because of the soul mate bond?"

Elias crumbles a napkin and leans back in his chair. "Like I said, she retains her memories because of the soul bond, yes. The compulsion, though?" He scratches his beard. "She said Sebastian tried, and it didn't work with him either. Maybe something happened when you healed her. Maybe it's something else, but compulsion is the least of your concerns right now."

I stare into the fire. Three days ago, my biggest worry was dealing with Father after my birthday.

"What will Sebastian do with her if he gets his hands on her?"

"The soul mate of Hamon's son? What do you think?"

I curse.

"Your father has enemies. She would be a nice bargaining chip."

"He wouldn't care. He doesn't care about me or what I do, as long as I join his ranks."

Elias laughs. "You don't think your father will find power in this? Breckin, there's something about her. Something different. She's not quite human."

The moment I smelled her blood, I had the same thought.

"I've met her mom. She's human."

Elias shifts, his face thoughtful. "What do you know of her father?"

Nothing. No one in town has ever mentioned Rachel Freeman having an ex-husband or Vivienne knowing her dad. I shrug.

"Her mom came home after college expecting. He was never in the picture. I'm not even sure her mom knows who he is," Elias says as his hand runs over his jaw.

My gaze snaps from the flames to Elias. "What makes you say that? How in the hell would you know anything about her family, anyway?"

"Breckin, the Freeman family has lived in Havenwood Falls for a long time. I've been here a long time. I know things."

"Is this about the Court? Are they involved with Viv somehow? I know what they do to people who anger them. I don't want her involved with them, Elias. She's—"

"I'm saying I'm an angel who has been here a long time for reasons other than you. I did speak to Ric about Vivienne's attack, though."

"The sheriff? Why?" The Court of the Sun and the Moon doesn't rule over us as angels. Their magic simply can't compare to our power. Elias has worked with them to keep peace, but why involve them with this?

"A girl went missing a week ago, Breckin. Whatever attacked Vivienne could be behind her disappearance. We can't keep the information secret."

"And what if it was something else? Something to do with us, or Vivienne specifically? What if the Court comes after her? If she isn't human, they will—"

"Breckin," he says my name sharply, reining my fears in. "Ric is trustworthy. We may need the Court's help eventually, but for now we can handle it on our own. He's agreed to let us deal with things as long as it stays among our kind." He watches my face and continues. "She was right to ask what the point of her being your soul mate is, by the way. There's a reason you were brought together. There always is."

I stand. I want to scream. I need to fly, to think. My wings want release. They want the freedom of the open sky.

"Go." Elias leans forward and jerks his head toward the stairs. He knows me well. "Take a moment, calm yourself. I'll watch over her."

I could use it. A flight to work off some energy. Watching over

Vivienne the last few days, even when in secret, has left me no time to breathe. My hand goes to my back, intending to yank my shirt over my head, but the sound of water in the bathroom stops me.

"No. I can't run away from this, even for a little while." I lower my voice. "Whatever I have to do to protect her, Elias."

He tips his head. "We'll need to end him."

"Then we end him."

Vivienne steps out, smoothing her hair into a high ponytail, and looks up. She catches me watching and smiles. My wings settle, my restlessness calming. She does that. Only her.

"I was thinking about what you said, and I realized something," she says as she crosses the room, and I twist on the couch to get a better look at her. "I watch you, too."

"You do?"

Her eyes shift from Elias to me. "You sit in the back at assemblies. You tap your fingers on the edge of your desk in chem like you're playing a song in your head, and you glared at me in middle school every time I caught your eye. I thought you hated me."

It clicks. "And you stopped talking to me," I recall as she returns to my side on the couch.

She lifts her shoulder and frowns. "I cried." Her hand covers her mouth. "Oh my gosh. I'd forgotten about it, but I did. I went home and cried to my mom because Breckin Roberts seemed to hate me, and I couldn't figure out why."

I push back my hair and inhale deeply. *I hid from her.* I spent most of the summer between sixth and seventh grade travelling with Elias. We came back, and when school started, I saw Vivienne in the hallway and nearly threw up. My stomach dropped and shook, like I was in a space shuttle. I'd chalked it up to a crush when it didn't stop after a week. Every time I saw her, I felt crazy.

I look at Elias. His mouth forms a small grin, and his eyes shine with suppressed laughter. "You knew," I breathe.

Vivienne's head whips to my "uncle."

"I suspected."

"Suspected? For how long?" I ask.

"From the first time you met."

Vivienne gasps, and I fish her hand out from the sleeve of her sweater and interlace our fingers. "Tell us."

Elias's grin drops. "I wasn't there. You were with a nanny at the time, Kathy I think it was, and she said you two went for a walk at the park. Vivienne and her mom were there. She gushed on and on about how inseparable you two were. It could have been two toddlers just playing, but—"

His eyes narrow meaningfully, and I pick up what he wasn't saying. *He knew. He knew she was different.*

"You think we were always connected, then?" Vivienne asks.

"I think you were. Like I said, soul mates are forever. Somehow you two were able to ignore the attraction. I imagine it was easier to resist because you'd felt it from such a young age."

Vivienne and I share a glance. There's no denying the attraction anymore. And there are no easy answers when discussing things pertaining to destiny and creation.

"If you suspected we were soul mates, why didn't you say something to me that first night? You made me think we could fix everything by erasing her memories." *Why is he keeping things from me?*

Elias scratches his beard and blows out a long exhale. "I hoped I was wrong. I wanted the memory erasure to work, Breckin. I didn't want to see either of you put into this situation."

His eyes meet mine, and they're filled with words he will not speak. *This will be trouble.*

He warned me that first night, but I thought he was worried about my healing her, or my exposing myself. No, he's worried for us. I give him a nearly imperceptible nod, letting him know I understand.

Vivienne clears her throat and shimmies—like she's shaking off a pall. "So, Elias. An angel who runs a business flying people on high adventure ski courses. It almost feels like an inside joke."

I choke on the sip of water I just took. For his part, Elias just leans back and snorts, his eyes watching Vivienne again with a gleam that I can only think of as pride.

"It *was* a joke. In a way."

Vivienne laughs lightly. "In a way?"

"Elias can't fly, Viv," I explain, unable to keep myself from wincing. An angel's wings are irreplaceable. They are their own life force. They speak their own language. How Elias manages without his has always amazed me. Vivienne's face contorts. I can read the questions she's too afraid to ask in her expressive eyes.

"It was years ago, a fight with things best left unsaid, for now," Elias says.

Unsaid, for now. Hopefully, unsaid forever. I don't want to have to tell Vivienne about all of the scary things that lurk about this world. She hasn't asked about other creatures, whether from fear or preoccupation, and I'd love it if she never had to find out. *Wishful thinking, Breckin.*

There's a sadness in her eyes as she looks at Elias. "I'm sorry." She offers him a warm smile.

He accepts her smile with one of his own. "It's not so bad. The business keeps me in the air, and I get to keep an eye on this delinquent."

"So that's how you ended up in Havenwood Falls? Breck's father asked you to watch over him while he's out doing . . . things?"

"Things?" Elias laughs, but agrees.

But that's not true. Elias was in Havenwood Falls way before I was born. He was here before he lost his wings, if I remember correctly. Why *did* he settle here?

THE HIGH-PITCHED SCREECH of Vivienne's window opening draws a smile to my face. Leaning against the tree outside her apartment, I maintain my focus on the parking lot and sky and wait for her to speak.

"You know I can see you even when you try to cloak yourself, right?"

She never disappoints. We've done this all week. I wait for her feisty little jabs like a hungry man waits for dinner. The scent of her freshly washed hair invades my space, and with a last glance around the complex, I turn and walk closer.

"Your neighbors will think you're crazy if you keep yelling outside at nothing."

"Breckin, go home and sleep. He's not here. It's been four days, and we've seen nothing."

She props her elbows on the sill and leans farther out. Taking the end of her wet hair, I wrap it around my fist and cloak her with me. "I don't sleep," I tell her, not for the first time. "And I want to be here. I feel better when I'm near you." I breathe her in before capturing her mouth with mine. She tastes like cinnamon toothpaste.

"Then come inside," she says against my lips, her tongue running over my bottom lip.

"That's not a good idea, Vivie." Her mom is at work, and the desire between us is too strong.

"It's a great idea, Breck." Her hands go around my neck, as though she can yank me in through her window.

Tucking my wings tight against my body, I climb into her room, shutting and locking the window before pulling the curtains closed. I still at Vivienne's proximity, my back to her.

"I'm not sure which I find more beautiful. You or your wings," she says softly for my ears only. Her finger grazes the edge of my left wing, and my breath hitches. She's never touched them. No one has. I close my eyes, yearning for her touch, my feathers straining for it. She moves to the curving slope at the top.

"I am an angel. I am not beautiful." My voice is as gravelly as Elias's. I fist her curtain as her entire palm pets down the length of my spine. The baby fine feathers twitch.

"You are my angel, Breckin Roberts, and you are beautiful to me."

I move quickly—grabbing her body and pinning her on top of her bed—with an angelic passion and need I've never known. Vivienne gasps, bucking against me as her eyes sparkle.

"You. Are. My soul."

Her leg hooks around my calf. "Do you know how badly I've wanted to touch them?" she asks with a breathtaking smile.

"You are my soul, Vivie," I repeat, lowering my face to hers and brushing her cheek and jaw with my nose, inhaling her scent. "I'm connected to you like no other."

She trembles beneath me. "I'm connected to *you* like no other."

I release her wrists from over her head. Pushing up, I brace myself with one hand and run my palm across her smooth skin. I've kept information from her all week, and I've run out of time.

"You're frowning. What's wrong?" Her warm fingers travel over my ribs and pull me down on top of her.

Pulling my wings in, I flip us over and hug her tightly. "I need to tell you about my father."

She lifts her head, her eyes scanning my face before she scrambles from my arms and sits beside me. I push myself into a sitting position. "Elias had to tell him what was going on here."

"Okay."

I blow out a deep breath. "You know he's not good. He's fallen, Viv. Thousands of years ago, there was dissension in the ranks, and it led to war."

"Among the angels?" Her eyes dip to my chest, and she leans over and tugs my shirt from where I keep it tucked in my belt. She arches a brow as she holds out the shirt.

"Yes, among the angels," I confirm as I slip the shirt over my head. "They were divided, some turned. The stories I've been told come from one side. Or I suppose, two—my father and Elias. They tell the same one, though. Mostly. They were thrown out of Heaven—many angels were—and for a while, they worked to gain their favor back, but when nothing happened, they fought. My father turned, and now leads other lesser angels in tempting humans to stray. It's his job to turn people away from living a good and righteous life."

"You're not your father, Breckin." She takes my hand when I stare at her with confusion. "You told me you were supposed to be bad. You're not."

"No, but I'm expected to declare my allegiance to him when I turn eighteen. I'm supposed to join him."

"And if you don't?"

Man, I love her strength. I hold her gaze as I admit the worst-case scenario. "He could end me."

"End you?" Her head shakes slowly. "You mean kill you?"

"Elias says he won't. Although he's never shown much fatherly care, he has some feelings for me. More than likely he'll force me, or make my life hell, until I relent."

"I don't understand. Can't you just live? Have some sort of neutrality? Go to college and be with me?"

I'd like nothing more. Vivienne's blue eyes fill with tears, and I hook her by the back of the neck and press her head to my chest. "I could try, but eventually I'll have to pick a side. Peace won't last forever."

"Why are you telling me all this now?" She swipes at her wet cheeks as she draws back.

"In order to keep you safe, we have to end Sebastian. Only one thing kills a reaper. Death's scythe, which, unless you have a direct line to him, we're not getting our hands on." Vivienne's hands go to her head. "But, I learned something before I came over. If a reaper is in a host body, as our guy is, then an angel blade will do him in."

"Where do you find an angel blade?"

My finger slides over her damp hair, taking a thick section and twisting it. "From my father."

READY, SET, LET'S GO

VIVIENNE

"So, are you ever going to talk to me about Breckin Roberts?"

My grip loosens on my curling iron, the metal coming way too close to my ear, as Mom pops her head around my bathroom door as I'm getting ready for school.

"Gosh, you scared me!" I unwrap a curl and set the iron on the counter. "What are you doing home this early?"

"I have seven months before my only child goes off to college. I figured if I wanted to spend any time with you, I'd have to come home before you left for school."

Guilt sucker-punches me. "I'm sorry."

She picks up the curling iron and steps behind me. Drawing a chunk of hair from my scalp, she sets about curling it, just as she did when I was younger. "You haven't been running, you haven't stopped by the clinic to help file. This boy must be pretty special for you to give up all of your normal activities."

"He is," I admit, meeting her gaze in the reflection of my bathroom mirror. "Do you need me at the medical center? I can come in."

"Not if you'd rather hang out with Breckin, sweetie."

See your mostly working mom or hang out with your newly found soul mate? What a choice. I fuss with the front of my hair, searching for pieces in need of the curling iron, as I carefully consider my answer.

"What if I bring him by?"

Her light brow arches. "Introducing him to the parental unit? Is he that special?"

My eyes roll as I smirk. "Mom, you know Breckin. You know his . . . Elias—"

"His Elias? Is that a term you kids are using these days that I wouldn't understand?"

"Elias Jamison. He's Breckin's unofficial uncle. We ate dinner with him. He's really nice."

Her face changes. A thoughtful and far off look glazes over her eyes. "Yes, he is nice. And yes, I know them both, but not all that well. I'd love it if you brought Breckin by the center. I'd like to get to know the boy who's convinced my normally rigid daughter to drop her schedule for an entire week."

"Rigid daughter?" I scoff. She raises her brow again, a silent "Are you going to dispute it?" and I give in. "Aren't you the one who poked at me for not having enough fun?"

"Not too much fun, Viv," she says, and I inhale deeply at the censure in her tone.

This week has been a whirlwind. My usual "rigid" schedule, as Mom calls it, fell to the wayside. My daily running was replaced by making out with an angel. My evenings helping Mom file charts and eating dinner with her at work were replaced by dinner dates in front of a fire with Breckin. Four afternoons spent doing our homework together, and getting to know each other, on a level other than the angelic, soul mate level.

"It's a good thing you raised me right." I turn and pilfer the curling iron from her hands. "He'll be here soon. Let me finish getting ready. How about we come by tonight? A Friday night date with my mom at a medical center? How could he say no?"

"Say no to a night with the Freeman girls? He couldn't." She slaps my butt on her way out the door.

~

I HAVE SO MANY QUESTIONS. Breckin and I need to talk before Mom jumps on him and interrogates him tonight. If he agrees to go. I should have asked on the way to school, but I chickened out. I should have said something before he left me at my classroom door, but my stomach fluttered and my senses swam as he kissed my cheek.

I've put off letting them meet because I was worried she would see just how strong my feelings for him are. She knows me too well. Now, before they meet, I need to sort things out. Things I put off because I was too frightened of the answers. If Breckin is my soul mate, what does that mean? We're seventeen. We're in high school. This isn't normal, being this attached to another when you're not even sure of yourself.

And he's an angel. He won't age much further—he's immortal. Will I be a creepy old woman passing the man I love off as my son, then grandson someday? I will grow old and die and leave him behind. My stomach turns. Am I thinking of a future with Breckin? Am I in love with him? Our souls are so in sync, it clouds all other feelings. It could be love, but it's too soon to go there. Soul mates or not. Isn't it?

"Buck up, cupcake. You'll see lover boy again in one hour." Zara knocks the back of my head as she takes her seat beside me. We've spoken less this last week than we have our entire lives. "You two are the real deal, huh?" Her words are dipped in resentment.

"Jealous?"

Zara snorts. "Of your hot boy toy? Totally. But I miss you more. He's gonna have to give you up. At least occasionally—shared custody?"

I smile. Just like with my rigid schedule and mom, I've disappeared on Zara this week, too. With a rogue angel out to get me, it can't exactly be helped, but she doesn't know that.

"Eat lunch with us, and we can work out arrangements."

"Really? He'll share you?"

Never. Breckin's words—*You. Are. My soul*—roll through my head.

I flash a coy smile. "What makes you think he's the needy one?"

"I've never known you to be clingy, Viv."

"That's because you've never known me to be in love."

Her face changes from wide-eyed shock to worry. *Why did I admit that? Was I not just questioning my feelings? I'm an idiot, because I know darn well what my feelings are.*

"You think you're in love?" Zara scoots her chair halfway into the aisle. "Viv, I don't want to see you get hurt. I know there's some sexy appeal to Breckin Roberts, but he's *Breckin Roberts*. Don't get your hopes up."

She means well. I push the leg of her chair with my foot, sliding her back toward her own desk. "I love you, Z. Everything will be fine."

If she has more to say, she's denied the chance by the start of class.

Halfway through AP Lit, my cell vibrates. I covertly slip the phone from my pocket.

Breck: My father is at the house. I have to go see him.

Me: Now? I'll come with you.

My heart races as I wait for his reply. He's taking too long. Why? A glance at the front of the room verifies I'm not being watched. I type again.

Me: Breck?

Breck: You can't. I need you to stay here. Stay in the building and with someone at all times, okay? I'll be back in time for chem.

I can't? Irrational worry, or maybe it isn't irrational considering what he's told me about his father, hits me.

Me: Will Elias be there?

Again, his reply takes too long. I lean down and grab my backpack, half determined to run for the exit. Beside me, Zara hisses, drawing my attention. Her brows dip over her eyes in a silent question. I shake my head and mouth, *I'm fine.*

Breck: Elias is there, Vivie. I'll be fine, I promise. I'll see you soon.

The remainder of class is a blur. Within moments of Breck's last text, dread hits me. I rub my chest, the emptiness I felt after he and Elias attempted erasing my memories coming back full force. Elias said I'd get used to it—the way my bond calls to Breckin's when we're not in close proximity. I'm empty, and he's not even two miles away.

Two sharp knocks on the classroom door stops us in the middle of reading a passage from *Heart of Darkness*.

"Sorry for the interruption. May I see Vivienne for a moment please?"

The pencil I'm doodling with stills as I look up. The assistant principal wants me? She lifts a hand and waves me over, before ducking back into the hall. Sharing a curious glance with Zara, I slip my cell up my sleeve and stand. The reading continues before I've left the room.

AP Lit is at the end of a hallway on the first floor of the school. To the left are exit doors with colorful posters advertising the Yuletide Ball tomorrow night, and to the right is a long corridor of closed classroom doors, and the Assistant Principal's back, as she walks away.

Am I supposed to follow her? What about my things?

The exit doors behind me open, a shock of cool wind and a beam of light shining into the hallway.

"Hello, pretty one." His rasping voice sends tendrils of fear curling up my spine.

THIS IS WAR

BRECKIN

*H*e stands in the middle of the living room, beneath the arched ceiling and before the burning fireplace, the owner of this house and my life. Or so he thinks.

"Father."

He does not turn. I didn't expect him to. "Breckin."

His profile is the same. The same face I've known my entire life. The face of a man who could be my brother. Thousands of years old and he looks like a frat boy right out of college. He looks like me, but looks are deceiving. Father isn't a college boy. He isn't harmless.

"Well?"

And he isn't patient. Leaving my wings out, I step farther into the room, nodding at Elias, who leans against a wall, arms crossed over his chest, the glare he wears for Father's sake firmly in place.

"I am told you healed."

I nod. His profile glows orange from the fire. I catch the way the muscle in his cheek flinches, and the silence grows.

"Where is she? This girl worth saving? I smell her on you. I smell her in this house."

My eyes flick toward Elias. His head moves a fraction, a slight shake as his pale eyes lower. I hold my tongue.

"You dare ask for my help, but you choose not to speak to me?" He finally turns his full attention to me. His amber eyes, more red in tone than mine, flash with irritation. "Do you know what you did, by interfering? Did you think your actions would go unnoticed?"

"I didn't have a choice."

"No?" He steps closer. "You risk notice, son. You have one choice in your existence: gain strength until you join me."

"That's a choice?" I scoff, anger unfurling in my chest. "I will not let her die. And if you don't help me keep her safe, you will be the one with a choice."

"Breckin." Elias pushes off the wall, his tone a warning, but it's too late. I opened my damn mouth, and I need to play it through.

"Do you think I'm stupid?" I ask them both. "I know you sense what she is to me. I know you know how important she is, not only to me but to you."

A slow grin works its way onto Father's face. "Perhaps there is more of me in you than I thought."

"Perhaps." I nod. "Or perhaps I'll do whatever it takes to make sure Vivienne is safe."

He stiffens, his head snapping toward Elias. Something passes between them. Elias lies for me all the time. *Does he know? Does he suspect Elias' true allegiance has been with me since the day he was forced to watch over me?*

"Yes, I imagine you will," he says after a moment, turning and tucking his inky-black wings close to his large frame. "This reaper, Sebastian. He disobeys his laws by remaining here. He lost his invisibility, thus making him dwell in a host. His existence is forfeit because he threatened my future."

"Thank you."

That is what I expected. He will say it is for me, for what I will bring to his leadership when I pledge my allegiance to his ranks. But I'm not fooled. He's curious to figure out why the Creator gave me a human soul mate. A human I'd known and been around all my life. I'd always understood bonds to be undeniable, and ours feels that way now, but why didn't it before? Why did it take her near death for the bond to click so strongly? I check the clock on the wall. First period ends in two minutes. "I promised her I'd be back in time for our next class. I don't like leaving her alone."

"I will meet her."

My wings bristle at his command, and I swallow hard. He isn't using his abilities on me, but he could. He could compel me to do his bidding any time he wants. It's what makes this all so damn difficult. "Eventually."

My pocket vibrates. Father cocks his head, his eyes following as I pull out my cell and answer.

"Zara?"

"Is Viv with you?" Zara asks breathlessly through the phone.

"What? Why?"

"Breckin, I'm aware of your reputation. You don't play by the rules, but Viv does, and if you—"

"What the hell are you talking about, Zara? Where's Viv?" I interrupt.

"She was called out of class, and she never returned. I grabbed her stuff and went to find her in the office, but they acted as though they had no idea what I was talking about. I figured you'd bribed them or something, since neither of you are in chemistry, where you should be."

"I had a family issue and had to leave campus. She was probably worried and is on her way here. I'm sure it's nothing. I need to go."

"Okay, but—" I end the call, shoving my cell in my back pocket and looking at Elias and Father.

Sebastian has her. She wouldn't have left campus. A growl rips through my chest as I swing at the nearest lamp, the glass shattering as it hits the wall.

GAME OF SURVIVAL

VIVIENNE

I can't breathe. We fly at such a pace, I cannot find a way to take in air without it being forced into my lungs. My eyes burn, and my skin pulls from the pressure being exerted. It's like the force of a roller coaster, but infinitely more powerful. I tuck my head into Sebastian's leather coat, hating the inferred intimacy, as I hang on with every ounce of my strength, praying he doesn't drop me from the sky to my death.

When I fear my body will be ripped apart by the wind, we slow, and his arms loosen.

I scream.

Opening my eyes, I cringe and duck as we fly through the dense forest along the rocky slope of a mountain. Are we still in Havenwood Falls?

His arms release me, and I slip. "No!" My hands and arms hold tighter, my legs stretching around his. "What are you doing? Don't drop me, please!"

My head jerks back, his fingers digging into my scalp.

"Can't you fly, pretty one?" His blue eyes shine as he laughs.

I peer over my shoulder at the ground below. Rocks. Jagged, loose, snow-covered boulders cover this section. I beg, tears pouring from my eyes as I climb his body, working to maintain my hold. It's no use. My muscles tire quickly, my sweat-covered palms slipping as we weave between trees. The moment my legs lose their connection with Sebastian, I anticipate the fall. Closing my eyes, I whisper Breckin's name. I picture Mom sitting at home, wondering what happened to her only child. I picture Zara and all my friends—will they find my body? Will I be another missing person like Heidi Bennett?

My eyes meet Sebastian's. "I don't want to die. Please?"

A smile graces his supernaturally perfect angelic face as he grasps my wrists and pries me away—as simple as plucking a piece of lint from his shirt—dropping me.

I have one moment to scream before I land hard and roll, coming to a stop when my arm cracks against a snow-covered rock. The snap of bone in my forearm sends pain throughout my entire body. The sound vibrates in my teeth. Biting my lip so hard I taste blood, I scramble into a ball and search the sky. *Where is he? Where did he go?*

The swoosh of wings is nearby. I push to my feet and run.

Tripping over limbs, tearing through bushes, and slipping on ice, I play hide and seek with an angel in the sky. His laughter trails me, and his shadow mocks me, never straying far from where I am. My toe snags a limb, and I pitch forward. I twist in time to save my arm from impact and slam head first into a thick pine. Warmth oozes down my face as white flashes behind my eyelids. It hurts. My broken arm, my weak legs, the throbbing in my head. Red drips to the white snow, and I lift my hand to the wound.

"Breckin?" I whisper his name, praying against all hope he hears me as the reaper lands.

Sebastian's shadow blocks the sun. His mottled gray and cream wings remain fanned out, like any moment he'll take off again. He's proud of what he's done—victory wreaths his face. But what is my cost?

"I knew you were special the moment I was sent to reap you. Death's orders are always the same, but for you . . . they were different. Your blood told the story. It has been thousands of years."

"What do you want with me?" I drag myself backward, my hand searching the ground for a weapon as I go.

"Had he left you to me, your soul would be free. I never considered doing anything but my job." He walks forward, keeping his distance as I push backward. "But he is the son of an angel," Sebastian says with distaste. "He interfered. He broke the laws, and he opened my eyes to what you are. What you can be."

Bile rises, burning my throat as the world spins. "What am I?"

The question barely passes my lips when snow flies, and Breckin lands, his body crouched before me. The muscles in his back flex, ready for a fight as his wings stretch out, taking up twice the space as Sebastian's.

"You," Breckin peers over his shoulder, "are my soul."

He scans me, verifying I'm relatively unscathed before focusing on Sebastian. My shoulders shake with relief. Using the tree at my back, I work into a standing position. Dizziness swamps me. I clutch the pine, my face pressing against the rough bark as I work to remain on my own two feet.

"You dare take her from me?" Breckin growls. "This will not end well for you, reaper."

Breckin leaps into the air, throwing himself at Sebastian, a flash of movement to my already blurry vision. The ground shakes, and thunder-like sounds echo through the forest as their bodies connect. Sebastian soars backward, twists, then launches at Breckin.

They fly through the forest, breaking branches and tumbling trees like dominos. Tangled limbs land on the snow a few feet from my position. I cringe as Sebastian punches Breckin, but Breckin returns the punch as though it was nothing. Back and forth they struggle. They're indestructible beings, fighting a cage match neither looks to win.

"Will she join you?" Sebastian drawls when they part, stalking each other. His blue eyes look past Breckin. "Will she turn her back on her calling for you?"

My stomach drops. Phantom butterflies within my chest flit about, tugging me toward Breckin while, at the same time, holding me back.

"You don't know?" Sebastian laughs. "He didn't tell you."

Is he talking to me or Breckin? My question goes unasked as Breckin's wing lifts, blocking my view, and more voices shout from above.

"Vivie, move back," Breckin orders above the others.

Breathing through the pain of my broken arm, I hide behind a tree. My legs refuse to move farther.

A moment later, a hand cups against my mouth as an arm wraps around my waist from behind.

"It's me," Elias says, picking me up off the ground and swiftly moving away from the fight.

"Elias? No. Help Breck. Where are you going?" I claw at his hands. His grip tightens, and I kick at his feet as he runs farther into the forest. He can't fly—we won't go far—but he runs with speed. Breckin's voice fades into the background, and my soul shreds, ripping a sob from my chest. Fear consumes me. "Elias, please. What if something happens to him?"

"His father is here," he pants, an edge to his voice. *Is that bitterness?* Elias thinks of Breckin like a son. It's in his tone. "Hamon will take care of the reaper. Breckin is fine. I need to move you to safety."

His words make sense, and he is attempting to help, but my body doesn't listen. I have no control over my reaction. My legs kick, and my head butts against his chest as I flail. A deep-seated knowledge that Breckin is being threatened has awakened, and my soul fights to return to her other half. Elias curses as I lean forward, throwing him off balance, and his arms loosen. Taking advantage, I punch at his arm and jump free of his grip. It was a mistake.

Falling to the ground face first, I land on my stomach, and black, all-consuming pain rips across my arm. Moisture and warmth immediately cover my skin. My sleeve is soaked in blood. I roll to my back, screaming in agony as I push the sleeve up. A bone protrudes through the skin.

"I'm trying to protect you," Elias hisses, falling to his knees and reaching for me. I flinch. Elias' face changes, his worry wiping away and leaving an unreadable mask. "I'm sorry, Viv," he says gruffly.

My head shakes. "I need Breck, please," I beg, willing my limbs to move, to run back toward the faint sound of yelling, but the pain is too much. My muscles lock.

"Everything will be okay," Elias says, lifting his arm. Everything goes silent.

WHEN IT'S ALL OVER

BRECKIN

*M*y father, an avenging angel full of malice and power, is a jarring sight as he lands in the snow between Sebastian and me. I risk a glance at Vivienne and find Elias dragging her away. Relieved, I focus on Sebastian.

"Hamon." Sebastian nods in deference.

Father glances my way. His mouth twists as he takes me in. I spit blood on the ground, aware the look I'm receiving is because of my weakness. My energy pulls, healing the wounds Father frowns down upon.

"You challenge the son of an angel, reaper?" He questions, his words full of distaste.

"I defend myself. Your son interfered with my job—"

"My son saved his soul mate," Father interrupts. He tucks his wings and moves forward. "You are inferior to us in every way. Did you think you could win something from me?"

The reaper's eyes go wide. His jaw slackens as he looks around the forest. Elias and Vivienne are gone. Father stands before him with an angel blade at his waist, and I'm ten feet on his other side. He's trapped.

He leaps into the air, but it's too late. Father grabs his ankle and throws him to the ground like a sack of grain as I rush forward. Sebastian scrambles back, but Father is a blur. The divine, even fallen ones, are more powerful than lesser angels, and before I can blink, Father has the reaper from behind, pulling him into a standing position.

"You damned her," Sebastian says between gritted teeth, glaring as he claws at Father's arm. "You should have let her die."

"How? How did I damn her?" I shout as Father jerks back, choking the reaper. "What is her calling? What do you know?"

Sebastian grunts, his lips parting, but his words never exit. My father's arm arcs around his shoulders, and the glow of an angel blade flashes as it slices across his chest.

"No!"

Sebastian's eyes glow, flaring wide, before closing as he crumbles to the ground, leaving the remains of the human host he inhabited before us.

"Why did you kill him?"

"Your soul mate was hurt." His gaze flicks over my shoulder. The snow is red with blood. "Find her and send Elias back."

My jaw clenches as I study him. There will be time for explanations later. Leaving him behind, I grab my phone and jump into the air in search of Elias and Vivienne.

"YOUR BATTLE SKILLS NEED WORK."

I turn at the displeasure dripping from Father's words. I'd assumed he'd be gone a while, taking care of the mess with Sebastian—even he answers to someone. Or so I thought.

Controlling my contempt, I nod. "There hasn't been much need for fighting here."

He killed Sebastian, with a simple slice to the chest. It was nothing for him, but it'll cost me everything, eventually. Including Vivienne.

"There will be." He walks to the opposite side of my bed and looks down at Vivienne's still form. She's a mess, with her knotted hair and dirty, tear-streaked face—but she is beautiful. And she is mine. I tense as he reaches for her now healed arm. The primal urge to challenge him for the audacity to touch her consumes me. Father or not. My face must tell the story, because he pauses, withdraws his arm, and inhales deeply. My teeth grind.

"You will prepare. You will train." His eyes never leave her face. "If you plan on keeping her."

Is that a threat?

"I have until April," I remind him needlessly. He can't bind me to his ranks until I turn eighteen.

"I can send fighters here."

"No." I stand, disliking the advantage he has with me sitting by the bed. "Thank you," I say, merely to appease him. "We'll be fine. I'm sure he told no one about her." *Other than you, of course.*

He doesn't realize I know. He assumes Elias is useless at anything other than watching over me, because he no longer has wings. Elias—the Dominion angel who ended thousands on both sides of the war between Heaven and Hell—a glorified babysitter. How does he not see it? Elias is the one who told me the reaper knew exactly who I was the day I healed Vivienne. Elias is the one who found out what Sebastian did with that knowledge.

The reaper went to Father and cut a deal.

When Father ordered me home this morning, I should have known. Vivienne's capture at school, the way Sebastian toyed with her in the woods—it was all planned. The only part that didn't go the way I, or the reaper, expected was the part where he met his end at the tip of an angel blade wielded by his supposed ally.

His betrayal doesn't bother me. Father isn't trustworthy. I've known this for years. His loyalty is to himself and himself alone. Sebastian wanted out of Death's servitude. He wanted a larger role in the things to come. I understand the reaper's motive. What was his?

"Why did you kill him before he could answer my questions? What do you know?"

Vivienne stirs, and Father cracks his neck, his eyes narrowing before he steps back.

"You have until your birthday. Elias will keep me informed of everything here," he says, ignoring my questions. I reach for Vivienne's hand, already dismissing him.

"Breckin, you owe me her life."

He's out of the room before I can speak, but his words send flames of anger through my veins. *I owe him her life? Yes, he saved her. Does he think he owns her, too? Will he use her to rein me in? Will he use me, to get his hands on her?* Vivienne's thumb rubs against mine, and I refuse to taint this moment with one more thought about his motives.

"You healed me." She licks at her lips and blinks several times. "Where were you when I broke my leg skiing two years ago?"

Pushing her hair from her face, my thumb smooths over the cut in her brow as I sit on the edge of the bed.

"Yes, I healed your arm and a pretty nasty cut on your forehead, but you still have some minor cuts and bruises." I place a kiss on her forehead and linger, my lips hovering over hers. "And probably a bit of a headache, thanks to Elias."

She turns her head to the right and winces. *Yep, there's the soreness.* "Are you hurt?"

Warmth floods my chest at her concern. This human girl could have been ripped to shreds by Sebastian, and she asks about me?

"Angel, remember. I heal myself."

"Elias hit me?" She confirms more than asks.

"You weren't cooperating, and I needed to get you away from the fight," Elias says from the doorway. His presence confirms Father is gone. I sit up. Kissing her can wait.

"I'm sorry, Vivienne. I'm sure Breckin can take away the pain."

She offers me a crooked smile before turning toward him. Her jaw drops. "What happened to your lip?"

"*He* hit *me.*" Elias points out, his fingers touching the split lip. "Then he warned me if I healed myself, he'd do it again."

Vivienne's blue eyes flick between the two of us, then she bursts into laughter. Grabbing a fist of her filthy, blood-stained sweater, I pull her into a sitting position and wrap her tightly in my arms. I kiss her temple, my soul quieting for the first time since it found her a week ago.

I GET TO LOVE YOU

VIVIENNE

"*W*ho could have predicted Breckin Roberts would lose his heart to a lass like you?"

"Gee, thanks, Z." My hip bumps hers as we watch Breckin walk across the overly decorated school gym for some drinks.

She giggles. "Every time he looks at you, I blush. You two are in so deep."

She has no idea. "The decorating committee outdid themselves. I barely recognize this place."

"I know, right?"

Trees twinkle throughout the gym. Everywhere I look, there are balloons, ribbons, and fabric in white and silver. Giant snowflakes and glittery stars cover the walls and hang in doorways and around the stage, where a DJ plays music. When Breckin asked me to the Yuletide Ball yesterday afternoon, I thought he was teasing.

"I PROBABLY SHOULD HAVE ASKED before my soul imprinted on yours, but do you have a date for the Yuletide Ball tomorrow?"

We're snuggled on his couch watching a movie, my head on a pillow in his lap as his hand combs through my hair. *The Christmas lights Breckin weaved around the mantle earlier in the week wink at us. Elias left an hour ago to work a little angel magic at the school so my attendance reflects an early dismissal due to illness. Breckin's father is gone, and except for a brief description of what happened on the mountain, neither Breckin nor Elias will tell me much of what went down.*

I roll my head and look up at Breckin. "The ball? No, I don't have a date. There's a group going stag, and I'd considered it, but that was . . . before."

"Do you want to go?"

"Right. Like you want to go to a school dance." *I laugh and roll back to my side, focusing on the movie.*

Twenty minutes later, Breckin's hand stills in my hair again. "Vivie?"

"Hmmm?"

"I want to take you to the dance tomorrow night." *My heartbeat accelerates.* "Nothing about being with me is going to be normal for you. I want to give you normal. School dances, prom, ice-skating at the park—"

I fly into a sitting position. "Wait. Are you asking me to prom?"

Breckin laughs, his hand taking mine and weaving our fingers together. "I'm sorry it's not some crazy social media–worthy request. I could plan one, if you need that."

"Are you kidding? All I need is you. And normal is overrated, Breckin." *I pull his face to mine.* "By the way, my mom is expecting us at the clinic for dinner tonight."

"That's reasonable. I should formally meet my girlfriend's mother."

"Yeah, you should," *I agree, kissing him soundly.*

"MAY I HAVE THIS DANCE?" *Breckin's lips tickle my ear as he steps up behind me, his hand curling around my hip.*

I take the cup of punch he's holding for me and turn into his chest. "You dance?"

"Drink, and come find out." *He winks and walks by, continuing to the edge of the floor and slipping his hands into his pockets. Waiting.*

I take one sip and set the cup on a table. Zara is already on the floor, along with everyone else we've been sitting with, but I don't care about them. Right now, it's me and my angel.

His eyes sparkle as I join him. My hands slip between his waist and arms, and press his back, bringing him closer. He keeps his hands in his pockets, a smile playing on his lips. I'm wearing four-inch heels, and still he looks down at me. *So not fair, but I love it.* I hold his stare.

After a moment, he caves, and I'm wrapped in his arms. His unnatural heat sears through my gold velvet dress, warming my skin. His chin rests on top of my head as he inhales deeply.

"Ginger and mint," he says with a touch of humor. His lips kiss my hair, before he pulls back. "That was how I knew it was you that day. I smelled ginger and mint, and I knew."

I press my cheek to his chest. "What happens next?"

I didn't mean to ask, but the questions linger. Sebastian's words won't let go of me. He said I had a calling. He questioned if I would stick with Breckin. He insinuated Breckin knows more than he's telling me.

Breckin inhales deeply. "We live. We celebrate being seniors, and we do all of those things normal couples do."

"Breck."

"Vivie." His fingers dive into my hair and tilt my head back. "I have found the one whom my soul loves." He quotes a Bible verse, as though every answer we need lies in those words. "We were not put together to be torn apart. I don't know what comes next. I wish I did."

I close my eyes and push away the uncertainty. He's an immortal angel. He can think that way. I'm not sure I can—I almost died once. He has until his birthday—four months—before his father returns and he's forced to join him. *What then?* I shiver, and Breck shushes me, like he knows where my thoughts turned.

Shifting, he lifts me at the waist and hoists me to face level. "All I know is that you are my soul. I will do whatever it takes to keep you and to call you mine."

Hugging his neck, I touch my forehead to his. "I have found the one whom my soul loves," I repeat as my lips touch his.

Our paths collided eight days ago, but our souls were destined for each other. Our future chosen long before we were born. *That* is what I know. How? There's no explanation, but deep within, something sings when it sees Breckin Roberts. And when I close my eyes, it tells me our story is far from over.

EPILOGUE

ELIAS

"**Y**ou ran out of the house yesterday," I call over my shoulder. He didn't make a sound, yet I know he's here.

"Oh? Did you miss me?" Hamon asks, and I turn. He leans against the open door to my hangar, his legs crossed at the ankles and his arms crossed at his chest.

I close the lid to my toolbox and adopt my own pose of insolence, propping my hip against my work bench. "Hardly"—I snag a rag and wipe the grease from my hands—"your son might, though."

"Breckin hates me."

"Do you blame him?"

"No." Hamon straightens, pushing his hands through his hair and stretching his neck from side-to-side. "You kept things from me, Elias."

His voice is filled with a deep-seated weariness. *How much are his alliances requiring of him these days?*

"I'm doing what you asked all those years ago," I say, recalling another night, seventeen years ago, when he also appeared in my hangar.

~

JUNE 2000

THE ECHO of footsteps in my hangar stills my hand. He's been missing for months, but I can't look at him—my anger is too strong. Yet, I have news.

"Phaedra's descendent had a child."

He stops walking. "A girl?"

"Aren't they always?"

"The father?" he asks as he rolls his broad shoulders back.

The question hits a nerve, a reminder of my failure, and I don't reply.

"You have watched over her line for two hundred years, but this you do not know?" He sneers.

"I was dealing with the mess you made, Hamon. I left her unprotected."

Stretching his neck from side to side, he steps farther inside, his wings bristling in the light breeze. Months gone and that's all he wants to know? His inability to speak of Phaedra's descendants aggravates me, but his unwillingness to ask about Breckin sets my blood to boiling.

I don't hide my irritation. "You have no other concerns?"

"Is her child the same as the others?"

"Human? Yes, she seems to be."

He stuffs his hands into the pockets of his dress slacks and releases a long exhale. "And Breckin?"

It's about time.

"Obviously, he is half angel. He is healthy." One of the Nephilim, not something Heaven likes having around. "The woman I hired seems nurturing. You should stay in Havenwood Falls for a while and spend time with him. He is your son."

"He is nothing. You'll watch over him as you do Phaedra's blood, and when he comes of age, he'll join the ranks."

I clench my jaw. "You will let him choose, though. Won't you?"

"The way we chose?"

Always this.

"We had a choice, Hamon."

"We were given less choice than man. We were locked out of Heaven."

Inhaling through my nose, I close my eyes and pray my words sink into his blackened heart. "There is time for redemption. You can change your ways. The wars will never stop. You can be on the right side."

"Tell that to Phaedra."

Everything comes back to Phaedra. I swipe the wrench I was using before Hamon arrived from the table.

"A demon killed her," I remind him needlessly.

"Because she was powerless."

We've had this fight for years. It is still pointless. I turn my back and return to working on my copter. Hamon's steps resume, and I peek over my shoulder, finding him walking to the open doorway. Leaving already.

"What is the child's name? Phaedra's blood?" He asks at the entrance.

"Vivienne."

His head bobs as his wings stretch out. "Watch over her. Watch over them both," he says as he jumps into the air.

I RETURN to present day when a grunt escapes Hamon's lips. "I suppose we should have expected this." He pauses, and I twist the rag and wait. "Them. Vivienne and Breckin," he finishes almost reluctantly. "More punishment—"

"Maybe it's His way of righting a wrong. His apology," I interrupt.

"Nothing good can come of them being together. What is she? A human with angelic ancestry? Something else?"

"She is your son's soul mate, and she is Phaedra's great, plus a few, granddaughter. She is family, Hamon."

"She is a complication. She will make him weak."

Like Phaedra made you weak? He has to be thinking it. It's in the way his muscles flex and tense. He's angry, because he sees himself as he was years ago.

I toss my rag down and meet him halfway across the hangar. "Stay in Havenwood Falls. Be his father and help me figure out what this all means."

The suggestion pulls a long sigh out of him, before he turns toward the exit. "I have a job to do, and so do you."

"Hamon?" He's leaving as he always does. Ignoring the salvation that knowing his son could offer him. Ignoring the forgiveness Breckin brings.

Hamon's dark wings spread wide as he stops. "I'm not ready, Elias."

"I'll watch over him, then. I'll watch over them both, until you are, old friend."

Without a response, Hamon leaps into the night, his wings an ebony shadow against the snow-covered trees as he leaves Havenwood Falls.

Breckin and Vivienne's story will continue in July 2018.

WE HOPE you enjoyed this story in the Havenwood Falls High series of novellas featuring a variety of supernatural creatures. The series is a collaborative effort by multiple authors. Each book is generally a stand-alone, so you can read them in any order, although some authors will be writing sequels to their own stories. Please be aware when you choose your next read.

Books in the Young Adult Havenwood Falls High series include:

Written in the Stars by Kallie Ross
Reawakened by Morgan Wylie
The Fall by Kristen Yard
Somewhere Within by Amy Hale

Awaken the Soul by Michele G. Miller
Bound by Shadows by Cameo Renae (Jan. 2018)
Inamorata by Randi Cooley Wilson (Feb. 2018)

More books releasing on a monthly basis. Coming soon are books from E.J. Fechenda, AnnaLisa Grant, Katie John, J.L. Weil, and more.

Immerse yourself in the world of Havenwood Falls and stay up to date on news and announcements at www.HavenwoodFalls.com. Join our reader group, Havenwood Falls Book Club, on Facebook at https://www.facebook.com/groups/HavenwoodFallsBookClub/

ABOUT THE AUTHOR

Michele writes novels with fairy tale love for everyday life. Romance is central to her plots, where the genres range from Coming of Age Fantasy and Realistic Fiction to New Adult Romantic Suspense. She is the author of the bestselling *From the Wreckage* series and co-writes the Paper Planes series with author Mindy Hayes.

Having grown up in both the cold, quiet town of Topsham, Maine, and the steamy, Southern hospitality of Mobile, Alabama, Michele is something of an enigma. She is an avid Yankees fan, loves New England and being outdoors, and misses snow. However, she thinks Southern boys are hotter, Alabama football is the only REAL football out there, and sweet tea is the best thing this side of heaven and her children's laughter!

Her family, an amazing husband and three awesome kids, have planted their roots in the middle of Michele's two childhood homes, in Charlotte, North Carolina.

Website: http://www.michelegmillerbooks.com/
    Email: authormichelegmiller@gmail.com
    Facebook: https://www.facebook.com/AuthorMicheleGMiller
    Twitter: https://twitter.com/chelemybelles
    Pinterest: http://pinterest.com/chelemybelles/
    Instagram: https://instagram.com/chelemybelles/

ACKNOWLEDGMENTS

I'm so grateful to the people who support me through the book process and life:

My husband and kids deal with me forgetting laundry, dinner, carpool, emails, and the list goes on. How they put up with me I'll never know!

My amazing crew of readers, bloggers, and friends on Facebook and "in real life" keep me sane. You make this solitary life a little less solitary, and a lot more lifelike. Thanks to **Mindy Hayes, Jessica Surgett** and **Jo Pettibone** for providing feedback on this story when it was new, sparkly, and still being fleshed out.

My core reader group over on Facebook, **Mindy and Michele's M&M's**: Thanks for being a sounding board when needed, book pimps when needed, and friends always.

To the Havenwood Falls family: This group continues to grow, but their generosity, creativity, and enthusiasm for this project astounds me. I'm so lucky to be able to write, and collaborate, with these amazing creatives.

More specifically, thanks to these ladies for creating and sharing your characters with Viv and Breckin:

Randi Cooley Wilson: Graysin Ravenal, Everett Weston, and Zal Purser

Kallie Ross: Scarlet Howe, Willa, Kase, and Ric Kasun

Kristen Yard: Nikki Morris and Max Cooper

Amy Hale: Mr. Zander

And of course, a final HUGE thank you to Kristie Cook for creating Havenwood Falls and making this all possible. I am in awe of your business savvy and ingenuity.

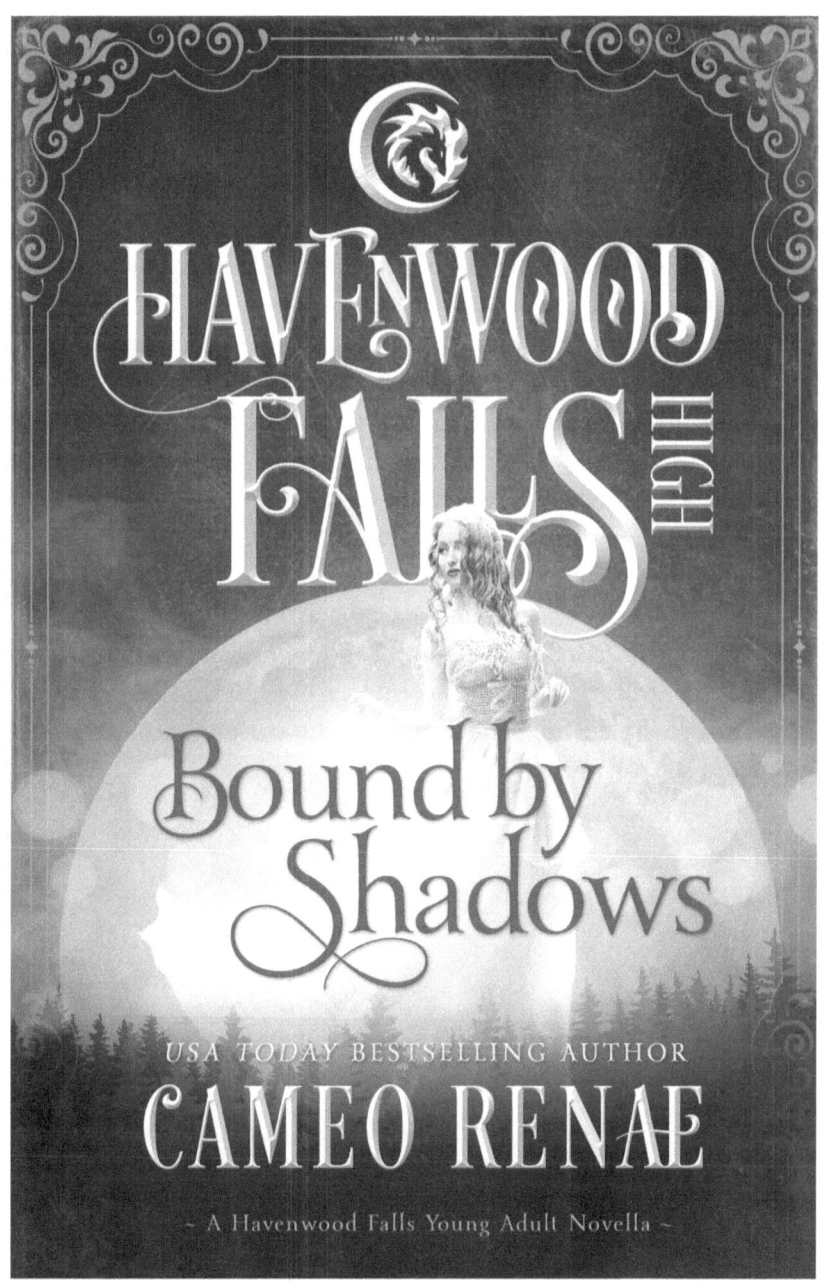

HAVENWOOD FALLS HIGH

Bound by Shadows

USA TODAY BESTSELLING AUTHOR
CAMEO RENAE

~ A Havenwood Falls Young Adult Novella ~

Bound by Shadows (A Havenwood Falls High Novella) by Cameo Renae

Eris Blaekthorn can't believe what she and her father find when two strangers come knocking on their door. According to the visitors, a memory spell caused them to forget a place called Havenwood Falls, including their life there and all the people in it. But when the strangers remove the spell, secrets from the past start to unravel.

Eris learns she has an older brother in the small Colorado mountain town. He's trapped in a coma caused by dark magic. But they don't know who did it or how. Her father agrees to leave their home in New Mexico and return to Havenwood Falls—a place he left to keep Eris safe. There, she learns about her family history and who she really is, which becomes the biggest surprise of all.

She also meets Rylan Gilles, a senior at Havenwood Falls High, and her brother's friend. He's beautiful and snarky, and their attraction to each other can't be denied. As events start to spiral and danger rises, Eris turns to Rylan for help in finding the person who spelled her brother so she can save his life.

BOUND BY SHADOWS

AN EXCERPT

Change was coming. I not only knew it—I felt it. Not just because New Year's was a few days away, but because of the newly gained sense I'd acquired when I turned sixteen a little over a year ago. So I wasn't hugely surprised when the doorbell rang in our quiet neighborhood on an uneventful Saturday night.

"I'll get it," I said, placing the last clean dinner plate in the dish drain, then wiping my hands dry on a dish towel.

My dad's watchful eyes were on me as I strode for the door. He was overprotective, and although I felt suffocated at times, I understood. It'd been just the two of us for as long as I could remember.

My father had chosen our neighborhood in New Mexico because it was safe and filled with dozens of cautious, watchful eyes. Especially the pair that belonged to the old lady across the street who moved in a few weeks after we did. She used to babysit me when I was younger, but not since I turned sixteen and pleaded with my dad that I was old enough to watch myself.

Old Ms. Gingrich—the Grinch—was a stiff and nosey woman who smelled of mothballs and strong herbs. She was strict and watched me like a hawk.

I wouldn't have been surprised if she was the one who rang the doorbell, hunched over, her wiry white hair in a tight bun, with some odd request for my dad. It happened so often, I wondered if she was going senile and thought he was her son.

As I reached the door and pulled it open, it wasn't the Grinch who greeted me, but two unfamiliar faces.

The first was a pretty woman with pale skin and short brown hair. The man standing next to her was tall with broad shoulders, dark brown hair, and chocolate eyes specked with gold.

"Can I help you?" I asked.

"Eris?" His eyes widened like he knew me. As he stepped forward, I stepped back.

He knew my name. How?

His strong scent wafted to my nose, woodsy and musky. A powerful smell for a powerful-looking man. I couldn't help but stare at him. There was something oddly familiar I couldn't put my finger on. The woman, I was sure I'd never seen before.

Footsteps pounded behind me. "I'm sorry, but we don't accept solicitors here," my dad said firmly.

The man's eyes moved to my dad, still filled with recognition. "Piers?"

My father stepped in front of me, pushing me behind him—a defensive move. Then, he went quiet as he took in the man's face.

"Garrick?" His expression twisted.

"It's been too long," the man replied.

The two of them collided in a hug, and I stood there feeling a mixture of surprise and confusion. My dad never hugged anyone like that, with so much emotion and intensity.

"Where the hell have you been?" my dad asked, grabbing the man's shoulders. "All this time, I—I thought you were dead."

"Dad?" I asked, trying to make sense of what was going on.

"It's okay, Eris," he said, turning toward me. "This is your long-lost uncle Garrick."

"Wait. What?" I gasped. "I have an uncle?"

"Actually, you have two," Garrick replied. "But I'm the handsome one." He winked, then laughed, turning his attention back to my father.

"Dad, why didn't you tell me?" I never knew I had other living family members.

My dad shook his head. "I'm sorry, Eris. There is so much I just can't remember."

"Piers, I know this is a huge surprise, and believe me, I understand." He turned to the woman. "This is Lyra Beaumont. We're here because—well—it's a bit complicated." He looked at the woman and ran a hand through his thick, dark hair. He was having trouble explaining their reasons for being here, frustration written all over his face. "We've come with bad news of a close family member."

"Is it Barney? Is he okay?" My dad's face went pale.

I assumed Barney was the "not as handsome" uncle.

Garrick shook his head. "No. Barney's fine. We're here about your son, Piers."

My father's eyes narrowed, then he glanced back at me, his expression unreadable. I shook my head and looked back at the man claiming to be my uncle. I didn't have a brother. That was the kind of thing someone didn't forget.

"Garrick, I don't have a son," my dad replied.

Garrick slowly reached into his pocket and pulled out a paper, then offered it to my dad.

Tiptoeing, I peeked over his shoulder to see an old photograph that had been folded in half, but I immediately recognized three of the faces. My dad, my mom, and me. But I was much younger. And there was someone standing next to me . . . a boy with his arm over my shoulder. I could see the resemblance. He had the same golden-brown hair and the same shaped eyes as me, only he was a foot taller and looked a few years older.

"You have a son, Piers, and if you let us in, I'll explain why you don't remember him."

My father paused, looking at the picture. I could see the tension in his jaw. "How did you get this?" my dad snapped, holding the picture up. "Is this a fake?"

Garrick held up both hands in front of him. "It's real. I assure you."

"Why, after all this time, would you show up and tell me about a son I don't have?" A deep guttural growl erupted from my dad's chest. "What the hell is going on?"

"Piers, I promise we'll explain," Garrick pleaded, turning to Lyra and giving her a nod.

Lyra quickly waved her hand in front of my dad and whispered a single word. I couldn't hear the word, but after she spoke it, my dad took a shaky step back. He shook his head, his eyes blinking rapidly several times.

Then, it was as if a switch had been flipped. His entire demeanor shifted, and his harsh expression was replaced with what I could only describe as understanding.

Could it have been magic?

I was no stranger to magic. Ever since we moved into this house, I could do things no normal kids could do. Like move things with my mind. My first real encounter was when Dad and I were sitting at the dining table eating breakfast. I was tired, and he'd asked me to pass the syrup. In my mind, I willed the syrup to move, and to mine and my dad's surprise, it did. He was not only shocked but immediately concerned and warned me —repetitively—to never, ever use my magic in front of anyone else.

And that wasn't all. Once in a while, whenever I felt really sad or frightened, a glimmer would appear—a small, bright ball of light, about three inches around, and when it came close, it radiated warmth. At first, I was afraid of it, but every time it appeared, it made me feel a lot better. Less . . . alone. I also learned that no one else could see it. So it had become my secret. A glimmer of hope and light that would come whenever the world around me felt dark.

My dad stepped aside, allowing my uncle and the woman into our living room.

"What's the news you came with?" Dad questioned, his arms crossing over his chest. I could see the muscles in his biceps tighten. He was ready to defend us, if he had to.

"I will tell you, but first, Lyra needs to perform a simple ceremony to reverse a memory spell that has been placed on both of you. Once she finishes, it will be much easier to explain."

"Memory spell? What the hell is that?" My father's arms lowered, and a growl rumbled deep in his chest. Garrick stepped back with his hands up in surrender.

"Piers, you know me. You've known me your entire life, and *you* agreed to this spell when you left Havenwood Falls, knowing full well what the repercussions would be."

"Havenwood Falls?" My dad shook his head.

"Yes. Think about it." Garrick approached my dad slowly, carefully. "There is a large chunk of your life missing. That chunk were the years you lived in Havenwood Falls with Aurora and your children. When you left, a memory spell—which is automatically placed on everyone who leaves the town—caused you to forget."

My dad shook his head. "I don't understand what you're saying, but I swear . . . if you do anything that will harm my daughter—"

"I know," Garrick said, his hands still raised. "You just have to trust me, Piers. Let Lyra do her thing, and we can talk after."

"Please, take a seat," the woman said, gesturing to our brown leather couch. She wasn't wasting any time, but I didn't sense any negative vibe from her. That was one thing I could pick up on in most people—if they had good or bad intentions—and my intuition was usually right. I guess my dad didn't feel anything negative either, because he gave me a nod and took a seat on the couch.

Lyra stood in front of us while Garrick paced slowly behind her. "I need you both to relax, close your eyes, and try to clear your mind," she said.

Right. Easier said than done with the gazillion unanswered questions they'd just thrown on us. And the fact I'd just learned I had relatives. Living relatives.

I leaned over to my dad. "Do you trust them?"

His eyes found mine. "I do. I have a feeling they're here to help and not harm."

I nodded, then leaned back. My dad took my hand, which helped me relax a bit.

"Wait a minute," I blurted, my eyes popping back open, finding Lyra. "Is this safe? Our minds won't be scrambled or altered in any way, right?"

Lyra grinned. "It's perfectly safe, dear. I promise there won't be any scrambled minds. I'm just removing a spell. That's it."

"Okay." I sighed loudly, wondering what kind of memories were hidden from me for who knows how long. "Let's do this."

As I closed my eyes, the woman began to chant. As she continued, I focused on the words, relaxed into them, and soon felt a gentle buzz in the air. My head felt tingly and light, like a weight was being lifted. Then, after a few moments, she stopped.

I opened my eyes and found her walking back toward Garrick.

"Is it done?" he whispered.

"Yes, the spell has been removed," she spoke softly. "It might take a while, but they should start to remember things soon."

"Thank you," Garrick replied with a nod.

"Wait," I blurted. "The memory spell—what exactly is it used for and why?"

Garrick sat on the loveseat across from us, his hands folded in front of him. "When you and your dad left Havenwood Falls, the memories of the place, the people in it, and everything that happened there were suppressed. Think of it as a type of amnesia caused by the spell. For me to explain why I've come, we needed to remove that spell. Lyra," his eyes traveled to the woman, "is a witch from Havenwood Falls, and one of the few trusted to reverse it." His eyes darted back and forth between my dad and me, watching us with great anticipation. Then, he clapped his hands together loudly. "So . . . is it working?"

My dad exhaled, pressing his face into his palms.

I was surprised he wasn't saying anything. He normally questioned everything. Why was he so quiet?

He finally sat forward and looked at Garrick. "Right now, all I have is a massive headache." He stood from the couch and began to walk toward the kitchen.

"Where are you going?' I called after him.

"To take something for this throbbing pain in my head."

"Just give the spell some time," Lyra said after him. "You've been gone for quite a while. It might take a bit to unravel all the memories. It's different for everyone."

My father returned a few moments later and plopped down next to me, his elbows pressed against his knees, the picture in his hands. His eyes were narrowed, studying the faces.

We all watched him in silence.

"I've had this emptiness inside I couldn't explain. A hole of sadness I could never fill," he murmured. "Now I understand where it came from. It was the place the memories once were. Memories of them." His finger traced over my mom and the boy in the picture. Then, he quickly swiped a stray tear that escaped his eye and trickled down his cheek.

I'd never seen my dad so shaken, so . . . emotional. He was strong, physically and emotionally, and not once had I ever seen him cry.

"I'm sorry, Piers. What Lyra just did will reverse the spell and return what was hidden these past seven years," Garrick explained, his brow furrowed.

My dad nodded, then closed his eyes. His head fell back onto the couch.

I waited again, for some lightbulb to click on in my mind and all my memories to flood back. But there was nothing. As time ticked on, doubt and frustration set in.

Just before I was about to say something, my dad's head snapped forward, and his eyes went wide, blinking away an invisible fog. He stood from the couch and stared at the man standing in front of him. I saw something in his eyes. Something I couldn't explain.

"You okay?" Garrick asked.

My dad nodded. "I remember."